MERCURY

Book 2

Lloyd Hall

CUPERTINO, CA

Wardenclyffe Series
PO Box 2918
Cupertino, CA 95015
www.wardenclyffeseries.com

Cover Design © 2022 **Abigail Spence**
Interior Illustrations © 2022 **Minna Ollikainen**

Mercury/Lloyd Hall. -- 1st ed.
ISBN 978-1-7373919-3-7

Dedicated to Clare, the best sister I could've asked to share a childhood with.

CONTENTS

CHAPTER ONE

QUARANTINE

The airlock door slides open and the air rushes out from around me. The vacuum pulls at my suit as I look into the room. There's a certain beauty to the old structure. Several marble tables sit within and a large planter floats by my face. I look up and see a hole in the ceiling leading out into the darkness beyond the ship. Distant stars speckle the space on the other side of the breach.

The gravity generators barely seem to be working in this section of the ship. Anything that's not bolted down is floating through the room like water. There are dozens of cups and various eating utensils drifting just off the ground in front of me, and as I go further in the gravity gets lighter. I brush the objects aside with my foot as I move through them, watching them drift further away. I'm careful to stay close to the floor of the ship as I slowly make my way through. The gravity seems to be almost completely gone, so I push off a nearby table and glide through the rest of the room. The feeling is so freeing that I bump right into the opposite wall. Whoops. I quickly turn around and pull myself into the second airlock.

I press the large red button on the wall and the doors close behind me. The air rushes in around me, filling the vacuum. There's still no gravity in this section but at least I've got air again. My helmet hisses as I remove it. I tuck it safely under my arm and take a deep breath. The air smells stale in here.

I float over to the other end of the airlock and open the bulkhead door. The manual wheel is slow to turn but I guess any automation this part of the ship once had is long gone. Feels like it's probably been sealed up for some time, but I eventually manage to get the door wedged open.

This section of the ship is unlike anything I've ever seen before. It's hard to put into words just how massive it all feels. I think the only other areas I've seen that have this much space are the forests down on the biome deck, but this feels completely different. The floor dips down in large areas and is covered in small, brightly-colored tiles, forming large pictures. In the center of the room there's a massive white stone statue of some guy with a robe on and wings on his feet. Probably an old captain or something. It has spots of random color but it's hard to tell for sure from a distance. Beyond the statue is a massive transparent ceiling. I can see all the stars beyond it, but unlike the other room, this one doesn't feel like I'm going to slip into space.

I push off the wall and move around the edge of the room. There's a large, cube-shaped object floating a couple feet off the floor and as I float closer I reach out and grab onto it. As I do, the cube lights up and a voice comes from inside.

"Well, hello there! Is there anything I can assist you with today?" the voice asks. It doesn't sound robotic. I move around to the front of the machine where the voice seems to be coming from. There's a panel lit up with a robotic face looking at me.

"Who are you?" I ask the machine.

"I'm Chip!" it cheerfully responds. I'm not in the mood for dealing with this.

"What part of the ship am I in right now?" I ask bluntly.

"Why, you're in the Lido Deck!" the machine responds before continuing, "Is there anything I can assist you with today?"

"What's the Lido Deck?" I've never heard of that part of the ship.

"The Lido Deck is where passengers can enjoy swimming in our state-of-the-art pool or relax with a drink at one of our dozens of poolside bars."

A pool? Ridiculous. "And what're you doing here?" I ask.

"I am here to provide passengers with an assortment of drinks and snacks," it responds. That's when it clicks.

"A VENDING MACHINE? YOU'RE JUST A VENDING MACHINE?" I yell at it. I push off and continue floating around the edge of the room, careful not to disturb any more machinery.

It continues speaking even as I move away. "Is there anything I can assist you with today? I have a wide assortment of snacks and drinks for you to choose from…"

I thought it was at least going to be something useful, like a ship's directory. Plus, I thought we had removed the AI units from most of the machines, but I guess this one must have been missed. Most of the ones that still have an AI unit are way more useful, anyways. I mean, after all, who needs an AI unit on a vending machine? I've certainly never heard of that before.

This room has almost too many details to take in at once. I'm definitely gonna have to remember this place for later. It might make a good hideout. Nice and quiet. First place I've ever been that doesn't have the noise of all the other people. I could easily spend hours here.

I float past long counters with small stools bolted to the floor in front of them. Behind each counter are signs with names of fancy drinks listed, and dozens of lights turn on as I drift past. Must be on automatic sensors.

I hold onto the edge of one of the counters and pull the top of my spacesuit open. My hands fumble on the closures but I eventually manage, pulling out the folded-up papers I had stuffed in there earlier. I lay them out on the counter, trying to keep them from floating away. Ok, the spot I'm looking for should be pretty close by.

I trace over the lines on the map with my fingers.

"So if I'm here… then it should be…" My fingers stop on one of the thick lines on the map. I look up to my left and see a wall. It must be right over there. I crumple the papers back into the neck of my spacesuit and push off.

Metal panels cover the entirety of the wall but one of them has a small handle which I promptly tug at. The handle clicks and the panel opens up, revealing a dark space beyond. I quickly slip inside. Small lights flicker on. They appear to be connected to a walkway leading out far in front of me. The faint lights get swallowed up by the darkness around me. Nevertheless, I pull myself forward and float along the walkway.

My spacesuit clinks against the metal railing and echoes in the darkness. Whatever this space is must be massive too. Suddenly a bright light turns on and what I had suspected is confirmed. I thought the Lido Deck was huge, but this new section puts it all to shame. I look over the railing and see the space stretching far below the walkway. Giant metal tubes span the entire height of the room, and when I turn upwards, they continue stretching far above me too. It's weird, everything in here looks completely different from the rest of the ship, which is all bright and decorated, while this area is cold and metal. Feels more industrial.

I keep floating along the pathway and continue past more of these tubes. As I get closer to each one, I hear things moving inside. The closest sounds like it's got water flowing, others sound like air, and some make sounds I couldn't begin to identify.

Further along, more of these metal tubes stretch out in all directions. I duck underneath one that's sitting just above the walkway, blocking my path. When I come up on the other side of the tube I see the end of the walkway in the distance. It ends at a large sphere with hundreds of metal tubes coming off of it.

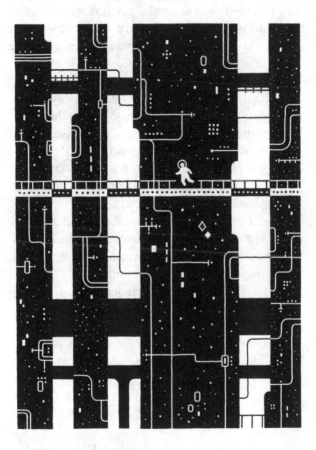

I keep pulling myself along with one arm, my helmet still neatly tucked under my other, which admittedly is getting a little sore but I'm almost at the end. I reach where the walkway meets this sphere and there's a thick metal door. I pull and it slams open, the noise echoing loudly behind me.

The interior of this room feels completely bland, unlike the mechanical walkways outside. And it's small. Like no bigger than my bedroom, and cleaner too. All the surfaces are bright white and dim lights illuminate the space. I kick off the doorway and float towards the only thing in the room — a small pedestal right in the middle.

I grab onto the pedestal and find a digital screen on the top. Another AI interface pings to life as soon as my glove touches the panel. A digital face stares up at me.

"Please enter user credentials," the panel says. I hold up an ID badge. There is a soft ping. "Credentials accepted. Welcome, First Officer Inez," the panel responds. A series of commands appear on the panel. START DRIVE. STOP DRIVE. DRIVE DIAGNOSTIC. OPEN WARP CONTAINER. CLOSE WARP CONTAINER. DRIVE INFORMATION.

"Please choose a command," the panel says.

"Start Drive?" I say.

"Drive unable to start. System error," the panel responds.

"Well, you're about as useful as the vending machine," I tell it. "How about Stop Drive?"

"Drive unable to stop. System error," the panel responds. Strike two.

"Then let's try door number three. What about Drive Diagnostic? Oh, let me guess—"

"Unable to run Drive Diagnostic. Fatal system error."

"Oh, that's new. So it's fatal now?" I respond. I really don't have the patience to be around AI. "What about Open Warp Container? Or can't you do that either?"

"Warp container opening." The machine pings.

"You're finally going to do something?" The top of the pedestal slides open, revealing a hexagonal hole. There are random cables and wires inside that don't seem to be hooked up to anything. I reach in and pull out some of the wires, but the ends are completely melted. What was supposed to be in here?

BUZZ BUZZ BUZZ. A blaring alarm fills the room and red lights flash the second I grab the cables. A voice comes over the automated system.

"INTRUDER ALERT. THIS AREA HAS BEEN QUARANTINED BY THE CAP-

TAIN. INTRUDER ALERT. RESTRICTED AREA."

Shit.

"YOU WILL BE ZZZZZ." The recording cuts off. Ok. Now what? Escape, right? The only way out is the way I came in. I kick off the pedestal and float back towards the door. I can't even begin to think what will happen to me if I get caught. The captain would probably throw me off the ship herself.

I pull myself back along the walkway, past the large metal tubes. When I finally reach the panel that I came through, I squeeze my way out and shut it tightly behind me. Maybe they won't be able to figure out that I went back there too.

This would all be so much quicker if this part of the ship still had its gravity. The entire Lido Deck echoes with the alarms and bright red lights flash. I push myself toward the long counters again, this time grabbing the stools to pull myself along like a ladder. As my fingers touch them, the AI bartenders spring to life.

"So, what'll it be?" one of them says.

"You look like you could use a drink," another chimes in. Probably true but hardly the time or place.

"Might I suggest a cosmo?" another says. Well, so much for making it out of here quietly. This place, which used to be so peaceful, suddenly turned into a virtual orchestra. I guess it was too good to be true. Maybe the next time I come back everything will have been shut off. I push away from the counters.

"Hi, I'm Chip! Can I interest you in a refreshment?" the large vending machine says as I float past it to the door.

"Not the time, Chip!" I shout back.

I shut the bulkhead behind me and quickly attach my helmet, trying not to get my hair caught as I put it back on, which is a lot tougher to do when you're rushing. Helmet on, I press the button and the air is removed from the chamber. The tug of the vacuum pulls on my suit again and I look through the other door into the space beyond. Floating plates and utensils still fly around, the other airlock beyond them on the opposite side. Just have to make it over there and then I'll be back in the ship. I can disappear once I make it back to the places I know.

I open the second bulkhead, move through and close it behind me, making sure it locks tightly. I place my feet on the door and quickly push off, propelling myself through the room again, staring at the open space in the ceiling the entire way. The hull of the ship looks like it was ripped away violently. I've never heard what happened to this part of the ship. And this wasn't exactly a productive search.

I turn my head to look at the opposite air-lock as the gravity starts to pull me to the floor. My heart sinks. There are three people standing around the airlock in bright green suits. I twist in place, trying to get to the floor but they're already surrounding me by the time I brush against the ground. Seconds later my hands are behind my back and I'm dragged into the airlock. Back in full gravity, I hear the door close behind me as I'm pinned to the ground.

The air rushes back into the room as handcuffs snap around my wrists. They pull me up to my feet and remove my helmet.

"Took you guys long enough," I say to them. Their helmets are opaque but I can tell they're not smiling with me. One of the ones who's not holding me by the handcuffs opens the opposite airlock door. They escort me back onto the part of the ship I'm familiar with.

"You guys know they've still got some AIs in there, right? You should really go take a look at that," I say as they lead me down the hallway. No response. Not a very cheery bunch. "So where are you taking me this time?"

Finally, one of them responds. "You're to be brought in front of the captain. She'll be the one to decide what to do with you." I'm pretty sure that's Harry, one of the chief security officers.

"So you're taking me to see her?"

"No. The captain has other matters to attend to. You will be confined to the Proscenium until it is time for you to be seen," he responds. They continue leading me down hallways to holding. Damn. I've always hated it in there.

CHAPTER TWO

THE BRIG

"You should get some entertainment in here," I shout into the empty room. No answer. It always feels like someone just closed this whole room off and completely forgot about it. Honestly, I doubt anyone's ever actually used it for anything other than keeping me locked up.

"Like maybe some games?" I continue. No answer again. I walk around the edges of the room and run my hands over the cold marble columns along the walls. It's kind of a shame no one uses this place for anything, though. I bet it actually looked really nice at one point. I look up at the only thing casting light into the room, an old chandelier. Almost all the lights inside are burned out, save for a handful of bulbs that cast a dim glow over all the old, velvet-covered seats below.

I stop in front of one of the paintings on the wall. It depicts a tall, white building on a cliffside, but the details are faded and hard to see. Every time I'm stuck in here, I can't stop looking at it. The wall it's on is crumbling and I can see the metal of the ship where it's fallen away. That's probably why this whole room is so dusty.

It feels like I've already been in here for ages. Is the captain really so busy she can't come down? Or is that just an excuse not to come see me? What could possibly keep her busy for so long? And I mean, the time would pass a little quicker if there was something to do. Even some music would probably help. Actually, that's a great idea, I bet music would sound amazing in here. This room's got a good echo to it. I hum quietly to myself and think about my adventure to the Lido Deck.

How long has that area of the ship has been quarantined? In the twenty-one years I've lived here I honestly can't remember a time it's ever been open. It certainly feels like it hasn't been touched in a very long time. I thought I could find some answer to why it was quarantined. I mean, other than the giant hole in the side of the ship. But apart from that everything seems to be in working order over there. And they could just build a new walkway through that section of the ship. I like to imagine what could be done with that amount of space. The rest of the ship is starting to feel crowded. Might be nice to have a little more room for people to hang out in.

I continue to look at the large paintings on the walls as I walk around, stopping in front of another. It's a group of people all wearing some kind of uniform. Looks pretty old but I don't recognize any of them from history class. There's a small plaque below that reads '*PHOEBE*'.

"Hm, wonder what that means," I say as my mind drifts back to the quarantined area. I thought at least the part with the walkway or that weird empty room would've been interesting, but nope, not a thing there either. For an adventure that got me locked in the brig it sure doesn't feel like I've got anything to show for my expedition.

I sit down in one of the chairs near the edge of the room and close my eyes. I can see the emptiness of space again. I don't know why that's sticking with me so much. I guess it's just different seeing it with nothing between me and the infinity beyond. It's a completely different feeling than looking through one of the windows of the ship. Like at any point I could just drift out into the void and never be seen again.

With my eyes closed, I focus on listening to what's around me. I hear the hum of the ship's electrical systems, a murmur of voices from somewhere in the distance, and random

metal rattling. All these parts of the ship are so familiar, like an extension of myself.

I hear a noise from behind me and turn to see the large doors at the back of the room open. The same guards as before enter, this time without their helmets. Two of them stand by the doors as Harry comes in with a tray. I guess they've learned their lesson about leaving that door open while I'm here. My last escape was pretty spectacular, if I do say so myself.

"I knew it was you, Harry!" I joke to him. He does not respond. Classic Harry. He's caught me more times than I can count. I almost think of him as a friend at this point. He doesn't think of me the same. He drops the tray of food near me before turning around and leaving the room.

"Not even gonna say goodbye?" I shout as the doors close behind him. I walk over to the food; it looks completely unappealing. The food has been getting worse over the past few years. Or maybe I'm just tired of always eating the same stuff. Wouldn't it be nice to get something new for a change?

I pick at the meal and eat a couple of disappointing bites before putting the tray down. I get up from my chair and pace around, tapping my fingers on the edges of all the old pianos as I walk by them. I tap the keys on one and it plays a horrible sound. I guess this is where all the ship's pianos come when they're out of tune. Seems to be a room full of things that no one wants to deal with. Like a piano graveyard. Oh! Maybe that's what I can call this room. That's a good name.

Suddenly there's a bright light in front of me. My eyes adjust and I see a figure standing on the stage in a spotlight. The captain, dramatic as always.

"Hello, Lucy," she says.

I don't respond to her greeting. Her face looks tired, emotionless and cold, but her uniform still looks pressed, clean, and perfect. Of course it would. Can't have her uniform look bad, right? I notice a faint static around her hair and that's when I realize she's not standing in a spotlight, she's using a hologram.

"Couldn't even bother to show up in person?" I walk around to the front row of seats and flop dramatically into one of them. Dust from the chair flies up around me and I stifle a sneeze.

She paces around and the clang of her metal foot echoes even through the hologram. "It's more complicated than that."

"That's what you always say." I look up at the chandelier again.

"I can't come running every time you get in trouble. I've got work to do," she explains.

"Just like always."

She shakes her head, clearly preparing for the same argument we've had… I don't even know how many times now. "There are dozens of problems on this ship that I have to deal with."

"Like me?" I hear the annoyance in my voice.

"Well, you're certainly one of them," she snaps. She doesn't mean to say it. I can tell by the flutter of regret that passes over her features, the crinkle of her brow and the hard press of her lips. Then she takes a breath and continues, "I'm sorry. I didn't mean it like that."

Her shoulders sink lower as she rubs her temples. I know she has a lot to deal with, it's not like I'm oblivious. It's been this way for as long as I can remember, and that's the problem. She's the captain of the *Mercury* first, my mother second. If that.

"Sure," is all I bother to answer.

"How did you even find out about that part of the ship?" she asks.

"What part of the ship?"

"You know what part I'm talking about. I can't even begin to imagine how you found it." She stares me down and I have a strong feeling she already knows where I learned about it.

I pull the old papers out of my spacesuit and hold them up. "Found these."

She sighs and shakes her head again. "You had no right to go through my stuff, Lucy."

"Why did you even have these in the first place?" I pry. Sure, it's not uncommon for a captain to have blueprints of the ship, but these papers are old, definitely from before she made Captain. I found them by chance. I'd been looking for photographs of my father, just some glimpse into what he was like, maybe even an old recording of him. Instead, I'd found these, crumpled at the bottom of a box at the back of her closet, buried under an old spacesuit. There were nearly-faded pencil marks on the papers, a faint scrawl that was barely readable but that I knew wasn't my mother's handwriting. A wistful part of me hoped it had been my father's and that if I followed the notes it might lead me to some answers. But the quarantined deck left me only with more questions.

"It's absolutely none of your business where I got those," she says. "You will return them immediately."

"No. I want to know," I argue, refusing to let her off on this one. "After all, you're hiding away secret parts of the ship from everyone."

"Look, you don't understand what you're poking your nose into," she says, her tone getting sharp again. "You really shouldn't have gone in there. Did it ever occur to you that there was a reason why we shut that part of the ship off?"

"I'm sure there was, and I'd love to know."

She pinches the top of her nose and closes her eyes, as if easing away a headache. When she opens them again, she looks even more tired. "You took my old ID card, didn't you?"

I pull it out of my suit and smirk. "Yup."

"I guess that means I should start locking my room."

"If you'd like," I say. Like I wouldn't be able to get into a locked room.

"Why were you even looking for that stuff?" she asks.

For a moment I almost mention him. I almost tell her I was looking for traces of my father, the man she's told me nothing about beyond the fact that he died before I was born. But I change tack and see if I can get answers to a different question, one she's more likely to answer. "Because of the rumors."

She looks puzzled. "What rumors?"

"That the ship isn't moving anymore."

"Oh, those rumors," she says.

"They're true, right? Everyone can see the stars around us. They haven't moved in years."

She shrugs as if it's unimportant, like we're discussing whether the bedsheets have been changed and not whether we're stranded in space. "You shouldn't listen to everything you hear."

"But if it's true I want to help! I found all those papers, didn't I?"

"And you're in massive trouble for that," she snaps.

"I even found my way to that secret empty room," I go on. "I followed the map and saw what you've been keeping secret all these years."

"Stop."

"And what's with that weird deck?"

"Lucy, stop—"

"And then there's that giant hole in the side of the ship. I mean what's all that about?"

"I SAID STOP," she shouts, and her voice bounces off the walls. Her tone steals the next words from my lips and I freeze. She's yelled before, many times, but never like that. It didn't sound like anger, it was more like… pain. And I can see it on her face too. Even via the hologram, I can see tears welling in her eyes and the tremble of her lips as if she's holding back a sob.

I swallow hard and take a quiet breath. "What did I say?

"You shouldn't have gone there, Lucy."
She sounds tired again. No, more than tired.
Defeated.

I know that I should stop, that I've already pushed it too far, but I can't, not when
I'm this close. "There has to be something we
can try to get the ship going again, right?"

"No," she responds quietly.

"Maybe it just needs more power? Or
what if we find a way to build a new engine?"

"Trust me, those aren't options. Don't
you think we've tried everything we could
possibly think of?"

"But there has to be more we can do! We
can't just give up," I say loudly as I stand up
on my chair.

My mom stares at me for a long moment
before speaking again. "You really are the
spitting image of him." She holds my gaze for
a fraction of a second before turning away.

"So you've said." The only time she ever
brings him up is to make that comparison, but
she never elaborates, no matter what I ask.
"Does this have something to do with him?"

"I'm not having this conversation with
you," she says, shaking her head, resolute as
always.

I groan and press my fingers into my
temples. "Oh, come on, you're going to have
to talk about him someday."

"I've talked about him—"

"Barely! All I know is that he was killed in an accident—"

"Do you think it's easy for me to talk about losing your father?"

"Do you think it's easy knowing nothing about him? You haven't told me anything! What about the good times?"

"Lucy, I'm tired. I don't have the energy for this right now."

"Please, come on." I was close, I know it. She was almost ready to open up this time. She turns towards me, wiping some tears from her eyes, and I know we're done.

"I have to get back to work now." She straightens her posture, adding a few more inches to her height. "I'll come check on you later tonight."

"Wait, so you're not gonna let me out?"

"No, not yet."

"But how can you not let me—" I'm cut off as she holds her hand up in front of her. She turns her head to face something I can't see.

"What do you mean?" she asks in a panic. There is a pause. "WAIT, WHAT?" she screams at something I cannot see.

And that's when I feel something I've never felt before. The entire ship begins to rock back and forth. Throughout my entire life on this ship, I've never felt it move like this. In fact, I have never felt it move at all. It

always kind of just smoothly drifted along.
The lights in the room flicker too. This can't
be good. I look back at the hologram just in
time to see static as it fades out before cutting
off completely.

What the hell just happened?

The ship lurches forward. A blaring alarm
rings throughout the room. Sounds like the
same kind of alarm that I set off earlier today.
At least this time it wasn't who caused it.
I hope. Unless I broke something in that
quarantined section of the ship? But for some
reason, this feels bigger than that. What could
I have done that would make the whole ship
shake?

The lights flicker again. I can see a couple of new cracks in the wall near me. Must
have happened when the ship lurched forward. I look down the room and see more
cracks forming on the other walls too. Just as
I'm examining them, the gravity generator
turns off. Why would they turn it off? I've
never known them to do that before. In fact,
the only place I've ever been without the artificial gravity was the quarantined section of
the ship. With the gravity off, I start to float
up toward the ceiling. I see my tray of food
floating up next to me. Oh well, not like I was
going to finish it anyways.

I twist in place, trying to get myself facing the ceiling but it does nothing. I can't

seem to get myself facing any direction that I actually want to. I hear a soft chime before a voice comes on over the ship's speakers. It barely cuts through the sound of the alarms.

"Attention, residents of the *Mercury*. We are experiencing some minor system issues. We are currently working to restore all systems," the captain's voice says. Guess she had bigger fish to fry. "You may experience slight power fluctuations as well as loss of gravity," she continues.

"Loss of gravity? No shit!" I scream into the room. The lights of the chandelier go out as it slams into the ceiling. "Well that's probably not good."

"Please follow all appropriate safety procedures as outlined in our emergency response plans." The transmission finishes with its signature chime. I think back to the safety procedures. What did it say to do without gravity? Oh yeah, make sure you grab onto something bolted to the deck, so you don't float around. I look back down at the chairs bolted to the floor. I guess I kinda missed my chance on those.

There's sparking from the shattered chandelier. Every couple of seconds the sparks light up the room with arcs of electricity. Just enough to see the outlines of shapes. Not enough, however, to stop me from slamming into the ceiling and bouncing off of it. I reach

out and grab the opposite edge of the chandelier, avoiding the sparks coming from the other side.

That's when there's a sudden pull from
below. The gravity is back on and I'm quickly
dropped toward the ground. I hold tightly
onto the chandelier, trying not to fall, but the
force is too strong. My entire weight pulls
against my arm as I cling to the fixture.
There's a sharp pain in my shoulder and my
arm goes limp, causing me to lose my grip. I
fall down into one of the rows of velvet
chairs, kicking up a massive cloud of dust.
The cushion is soft but the armrests aren't.
One of them digs into my ribcage. I try to
move and feel a massive pain in my ribs as
my left arm hangs limp at my side.

"You couldn't give me some warning before you did that?" I scream out. Then it happens again. The gravity turns off and I drift
upwards. I grab onto one of the chairs with
my right arm but even that sends a sharp pain
through my ribcage. Then, just as suddenly as
it had turned off, the gravity is back on. But
this time it's accompanied by a loud crashing
noise. I look over and see one of the marble
columns has completely cracked apart and
fallen over. There are massive cracks in all
the other columns too.

While the gravity is still on, I take my
chance and run towards the back doors. I pull

on one of them. Locked. Damn it. I try the other but it's the same result. Wait, what about the balcony? I'm pretty sure there's another door up there. I run back toward the middle of the room and look up at the balcony. There is a door, and I think I know how to get up there but it's not going to be fun.

I crouch down and wait. The gravity clicks off again and I quickly push away from the floor. I float through the air. The large pianos have also begun to drift upwards ominously. I clear the ledge of the balcony right as the gravity turns on and I'm tossed onto the floor. I feel the fall throughout my body, mostly in my ribs. I also hear a room full of pianos crashing to the ground. I look over the railing and see the columns laying in pieces, filling the room with rubble.

The alarm seems louder up here. I look up and notice the speakers all around the balcony. No wonder. I rush towards the doors and try to pull them open. No luck here either. Ok, but how do I get out of this room? I look around for another exit of some kind. The lights from the chandelier flicker and I see a small air vent on the opposite side of the room. It's up near the ceiling, which is probably why I've never tried to escape through there before.

Suddenly I feel light again. I try to push off the floor but I'm already too far away from it. One of the pianos is floating near me, so I grab it and pull myself around to the opposite side. I rest my foot against it and push off in the direction of the vent, propelling myself forward. Not quickly but every bit helps. I pass by a shard of marble from one of the columns and it catches my shoulder, leaving a deep cut and a stinging pain. Gotta be more careful. Some of these pieces of debris are razor-sharp. The chandelier slams into the ceiling and the final light in the room is gone.

I reach out in front of me, waiting for the feel of the grate. I was moving directly towards it so it must be close. There is nothing for a second or two, then suddenly I feel it in my hands — a slatted grate covering the air vent. I quickly pull the grate off and begin pulling myself in. I'm most of the way inside when the gravity kicks back on. I brace myself in the vent, trying to make sure I don't slip out.

"FUCK," I scream out. There's a stinging pain shooting through my body and my ankle suddenly goes numb. I manage to pull myself into the vent and look down at my leg. My left foot is gone, probably taken clean off by a sharp piece of debris. My vision is blurring and I can barely keep focused. I drag myself further into the vent as a piano crashes loudly into the ground behind me over the sound of the alarms.

I undo my belt and pull it out from around my waist, my hands shaking the entire time. I try to loop the fabric from the belt around my thigh. Shit. I can't keep my hands steady. I take a deep breath in, slowly breathe out again, and finally manage to get the belt around my thigh. I quickly latch it and pull it as tight as I can possibly make it. The belt digging into my skin would probably be ex-cruciating if I could feel anything other than the pain from my ankle.

My head feels light. I must've lost a lot of blood. Wait. No. Not lightheaded, it's that there's no gravity again. I didn't even feel it happen this time. As I pull myself down the air vent, I can tell my foot is still bleeding but I try not to look at it.

Which way is the medical ward? It's close to the brig, right? I can't think straight through all this pain. I can still hear the alarm blaring through the ship. It's softer in the vents but not by much. Was it a left turn up ahead or a right turn? These vents should fol-low the hallways, right? I just can't focus right now. I close my eyes again and hear a roar of voices coming from the left. That must be it.

I pull myself along and gravity kicks right back on, slamming me into the side of the vent, stinging my ribs again. There's a light ahead of me coming through a slatted metal grate. I crawl towards it and feel a decline, which I start to slide down, trying to grip something but to no avail. My head cracks into the vent and all I see is bright light before I pass out.

CHAPTER THREE

METEOR

I wake up strapped to a bed. Where am I? I try to sit up but the straps across my chest restrain me. I look around the room and see several other beds crammed inside, surrounded by a bunch of people wearing green uniforms — the medical staff. I must have somehow made it to the medical ward. One of them notices me awake and walks over to my bed.

"Why am I restrained?" I ask him.

He seems thoroughly distracted by the other things happening in the room. "You were in pretty rough shape when you came in here, Lucy."

"Let me go," I snap. This seems to get his full attention and he undoes the straps across my chest. That's when I notice the bandages wrapped around my chest and arms.

"Those were only there so you didn't float off." He seems totally frazzled by the recent chaos, his eyes darting back and forth between me and the rest of the room. "We're still having a lot of issues with the gravity disruptions." His eyes glance down at my feet. I quickly sit up and look at my ankle. A polished metal foot extends from where my real foot had been.

"It's mechanical." I'm in complete shock. I can't believe they gave me a mechanical foot.

He tries what I can only assume is his best attempt at bedside manner. "Yeah, the medical machines were able to get that sorted for you in less than an hour."

"What?" I get he's trying but he's not really the most comforting person I've met. I'm still reeling from what happened.

"Yeah, once you burst through that air vent and passed out, we put you into one of the restoration pods to monitor your condition. I guess it was able to construct an artificial limb for you. It's been a while since I've seen it do that, actually. I'm a little surprised it still knew how," he explains.

"So, it's all good to go?" I start to undo the straps holding my feet down when he sits on the side of the bed next to me and places his hand on mine, stopping me.

His face suddenly drops its friendly demeanor and his whole tone becomes way more serious. "Not quite. You're not gonna be able to just get up and go with this new foot.

It's gonna take some time to get used to. And
it's not just your foot, you're pretty banged up
all over." I can tell he's waiting for me to say
something, but we sit in silence for a few seconds until I finally find words.

"But I've got to get out of here," I tell
him.

He shakes his head. "We promised your
mom we'd keep you safe down here while
this is all going on. And she is the one in
charge." He tries giving me a halfhearted
smile before moving on to another bed, but I
can tell it's entirely forced. I look around the
rest of the room.

I haven't been down to the medical ward
in a long time. All the staff wear the same
bland green uniforms with little caps on their
heads. The walls have large murals with
scenes from medical history, which I sort of
remember learning about back in history
classes. Portions of the murals are now ob-
scured by large medical machinery and
posters that have been hung all over the walls.
One of those machines must be the one that
helped fix my foot. I look back down at my
ankle.

It's surreal to think that I managed to lose
my foot in only a couple of hours. I can't
even imagine what could have happened if all
of me had been inside that room when the
shards of debris fell. I doubt I would have

made it out. Probably would've ended up crushed by a column or, god forbid, a piano.

I try moving my foot. The mechanical appendage responds as I wiggle my toes. There's a slight delay in the response, so that's gonna take some getting used to. I wonder if this is what it felt like when my mom lost her foot. She doesn't really talk about it but the distinct noise her metal foot makes commands order anywhere she walks on the ship. She even had her uniform tailored to show it off.

I suddenly notice there aren't any alarms sounding or lights flashing in here. I look up to where the speakers are and see a large cloth taped up over them and the lights. I pull one of the other medical staff aside. "What's the deal with the alarm over there?"

She gives me a small smile. "Well, honestly, we all know we're in an emergency and at a certain point it just gets annoying."

I laugh. Her bedside manner is a lot better than the last guy. She continues around the room to some of the other patients who are strapped into their beds like I had been. The wheels of the beds appear to have been welded to the floor, too. Come to think of it, this is probably the most people I've ever seen in the medical ward at once. Everyone seems to be in a complete panic.

I feel a lump in my bed and I shift the covers over. Next to one of the straps sits a wooden cane. They must have slipped it into my bed while I was asleep. I move it off to the side; I really don't want to have to think about using that yet.

Then it happens in this room too, the gravity shuts off and the reason for the elaborate bed setup and patients strapped down becomes clear. The beds, being bolted to the floor, stay exactly where they are. The patients also stay completely still, outside of some blankets floating up. The medical staff all grab the side of someone's bed and hold themselves on the ground while the gravity disappears. The only thing that manages to break free is a lone pen that floats upwards through the middle of the room. The straps across my legs hold me to the bed but I grab the sides anyways just to help keep me steady.

The gravity turns back on and the pen clatters to the floor. One of the staff walks over, picks it up, and returns it to their pocket. The lights seem to cycle on and off every couple of minutes along with the gravity. I try to figure out a pattern for their shifting but there doesn't seem to be one. I lay back down and rest my eyes. It's been a hell of a day.

◆

I'm awoken by the noise of a dozen people being wheeled into the medical ward. The room echoes from the slam of the metal doors as they swing open. I sit up in bed to see what's happening. The people aren't bleeding but they look extremely pale and seem to be having trouble walking. The medical staff rush over to assist and get them all hooked up to a series of breathing machines. As they're frantically trying to help, the lights cut out and I have a moment of instant clarity. This is my chance to get out.

I pull the straps off my legs and quickly roll out of bed onto the floor. My new foot clangs against the metal. Ok, definitely not used to that yet. I freeze. Waiting to see if anyone noticed. I peek up over the side of the bed, but no one has taken their attention off of the new patients. I slip the cane out from between the sheets.

The staff are using headlamps to see the machines they're working on during the blackout, so I crawl toward the doors of the medical ward and manage to reach them without anyone seeing me. I'm through the door just before the lights in the ward come back on. But when I try to stand up, my leg buckles beneath me. The new mechanical foot feels strange. It moves when I think about moving it but there's no feeling in it. It's like trying to walk while your foot's asleep. I lean on my cane and pull myself upright.

I limp down the hallway, leaning heavily on my cane as I go. My new foot taps against the metal floor with each step. The walking goes slowly but I need to figure out what's happening. The entire ship seems to be in chaos. The alarms and warning lights are back up to their full power outside of the ward, no longer having the blankets to muffle them, and I hear an announcement cut through.

"Please be advised that the entirety of Deck Eight has been isolated. For your safety, we are now beginning evacuations on Decks Seven, Six, and Five. If you are located on any of these decks please make your way to a higher level at this time," the captain says. She sounds so calm. And what happened on Deck Eight? Why is it shut down?

People are running around me. The medical ward and brig are both down on Deck Ten so whatever happened is about two decks up. I start walking towards the center of the deck and see the bridleway swarming with people. Everyone is crowded in a large mass trying to get into chariots to other decks. I've never seen it this busy before. There's no way I'm gonna be able to fight my way through the crowd in my current condition.

I turn down one of the streets and walk away from the centre hub towards the outer edge of the ship. I've seen smaller maintenance transports out there that go between the decks. I think I'll have better luck if I can get to one of those. I try to keep walking but my foot catches something and I stumble to the ground. I guess that medical guy wasn't kidding when he said it would take some getting used to. And not just that, my other foot is beginning to get sore already from putting most of my weight on it.

"Hey, you ok?" A girl about my age runs out from one of the buildings nearby. It actually looks less like a building and more like it was cobbled together from assorted junk in an attempt to look like a building. In the middle of the junk pile is a door and a large neon sign hanging above it in the shape of a purple flower.

"Yeah, I'm good," I tell her, avoiding eye contact.

She leans in, trying to get a closer look at me. "You sure? Cuz you look like kind of a mess."

"Well, that's not a very nice thing to say." I look up and make eye contact with her. She's got a big, dopey smile on her face and seems to be covered with what looks like soot.

"I just mean, you're in medical clothes. And seem to be having a tough time moving."

I look down at my clothes. I can't believe I didn't even notice I was still in this dumb med uniform. "That's my bad. Look, I have to go," I say.

She dusts her hands on her overalls and I see the soot shake off her. She reaches out and offers me the same hand. "Let me help you," she says as she lifts me up from the ground. "I'm Penny, by the way."

"Nice to meet you." I'm back up on my feet, even if my hand is now covered in soot. She lets go of me and looks me over. "Now I really do have to get down to the maintenance elevator."

"Wait right here." She runs back into the building she came from, and after a minute she comes out dragging a large bike hovering inches off the ground.

"What the hell is that?" I ask. I've never seen anything like it before.

She pulls a pair of big goggles over her eyes. "I'm giving you a lift, ok?" She climbs onto the bike and pats the seat behind her with a big smile. I get on. This girl better know what she's doing. I hold her tight as the bike lunges forward and we speed down the street. The rest of the shops are a complete blur beside us.

"We're almost there!" she yells over the hum of the bike engine. I can hear the absolute glee in her voice. Then suddenly I slam into her back as she pulls to an abrupt stop. The dark metal wall of the ship is in front of us. It always seems kind of creepy out at the edges. They don't take much care of these parts, so all the lights around here are burned out. I get off the bike and my leg still feels wobbly, although it's hard to tell if it's from the crazy bike ride or just having a new foot. Probably a little of both.

"I've got to get this back before my mom notices it's gone." Penny smiles again and takes off her coat. "Oh, and you better take this. Dress up those medical clothes a little bit." She wraps the coat around my shoulders and laughs. Before I can even thank her, she's back on the bike and blocks away. After she's out of sight, I turn back towards the wall.

The door I'm looking for is hidden off to the side of the street. There's a small keypad next to it where I quickly type in the captain's override code. The door slides open and I step into a large lift. Instantly the alarms soften. I can still hear them outside, but it's significantly quieter in here.

The interior of the lift has several large, wooden crates that are about twice my height. Who knows what they're even for anymore. They look like they haven't been touched in years. Probably just spare parts that someone left in here and completely forgot about. I look over to the control panel and see all the floors listed. I run over and press the number '8'.

A digital face appears on the panel and speaks. "Deck Eight selected. Is this where you would like to travel today?"

I roll my eyes. "Yes." Can't get away from these AI units.

"Please secure yourself and any belongings before travel," the unit says. There is a small ping from the panel. I look around for something to grab onto but there's nothing close. The door slides closed and the alarm sound is cut off completely. The floor suddenly shoots up and I'm knocked off my feet. There's a horrible screeching noise from the lift as it flies upwards. I think I preferred the alarm sounds.

The force keeps me pinned to the ground so I can barely move my limbs. Except for my left foot, which seems to sadly be the most functional part of me right now. The floor stops suddenly, and I'm thrown into the air. I try to brace myself, but it doesn't go particularly well and I slam back into the ground. That's the second time in two days. That has to be some kind of new record for this ship.

I pull myself up on one of the crates, which surprisingly didn't shift an inch during the trip, and look around to see my cane a few feet away. I limp over and pick it up.

There is another ping from the panel. "You have arrived at Deck Eight. Please be advised that this area is currently on lock-down. All unauthorized personnel should evacuate immediately," it says in a chipper voice. The door opens and I stumble out of the lift into the forest.

I stand just inside the entrance to the deck and take a deep breath. The air here is so much fresher than the rest of the ship. The trees loom tall above me. Far beyond them, I can see the clouds up near the roof of the deck. The usually white clouds are flashing red, an unusual behavior. Then it hits me; those must be the flashing alarm lights shining through the clouds. Certainly gives them an ominous feel.

I awkwardly stumble down the narrow path. Needles from the trees crunch underneath my mechanical foot while sticking to my other bare foot. I think the last time I was up on this deck was probably as a kid. We came camping up here a few times and my mom taught me all about the redwood trees. It's one of the few times we actually had fun together.

So what actually shut this deck down? It must've been something big for them to close off the entire level. Not to mention shaking the entire ship, which I've never felt before in my life. I keep walking until I catch a glimpse of something peeking through the tops of the trees. It looks like a pillar of black smoke. That must be what I'm looking for. I turn down a fork in the path and make my way over to the smoke.

The path winds vaguely in that direction, but it takes forever to get there. With a graceless motion, I climb over the short wooden fence and start cutting through the trees in a more direct route.

Almost immediately I regret this decision. My new foot doesn't take very well to the uneven ground and all it takes is a small log to trip me up. I tumble down and land roughly on a spot of moss, which might have been comfortable if not for the branch poking into my side. I roll off the branch and look down at my new foot.

My heart sinks a little bit. Something as simple as walking over branches used to be no issue for me but feels insurmountable now. I know the doctor said I'd be able to use it again, just like normal, but I want to be back to my full capacity now. After all, there's a disaster happening. It's the worst time for me to be out of commission.

I grab the cane I dropped and pull myself back up. Then I go slowly over the large branches laying around and come to the other side of the grove. I carefully climb over the wooden fence back onto the flat surface of the path and keep winding along toward the smoke.

Even though I'm nowhere close to it, the smell of burning wood reaches me. I haven't smelled something burning in years, but the scent is unmistakable. Usually, the ship's fire suppression system puts any fires out before they start. Even when my mom and I came camping here, we always used electric heaters.

I round a corner and find the path blocked by a massive tree that's been blown completely over. Wait, not just one tree. A whole bunch of them are leaning at angles. I look where the trees are leaning out from and see the apparent source of the smoke. Ok, I've got to get over that way.

Luckily there's no fence to climb over this time. The fallen tree took care of that, crushing it to pieces. I balance carefully on the branches as I make my way toward the smoke. More and more trees seem to be leaning outwards as I get closer. The upturned roots from one cast a dark shadow over me as I duck under them. It must've taken a lot of force to pull up roots that deep. I round one of the larger trees and that's when I see a massive crater sitting before me.

All the trees around it are blown out-wards, their red bark now completely charred and burnt. Small fires still burn softly on a number of the trees, putting out thick plumes of black smoke. But the fires aren't nearly as interesting as the large object in the middle of the crater.

It's massive. Almost as big as one of the ship's chariots. Could this be a meteor? We read about those in school, but I've never ac-tually seen one in person. I mean, where would I have had the chance to see a meteor before? I think back to the pictures in the schoolbooks. Meteors are usually smooth and shiny, but this object doesn't look anything like that.

In fact, it looks more like a piece of black paper that someone has crumpled into a ball, with sharp, jagged edges everywhere. And where could it have come from? I look up and see a massive hole in the cloud layer, and be-yond that, a hole in the deck above. It must've punched right through the outer hull and the upper decks to end up crashing here. But I still can't even imagine the sheer force it must've taken to break through our ship's outer hull. They told us in school nothing in the universe was as strong as that. So what could this possibly have been?

I start climbing down into the crater to get a better look at it. The ground feels warm against my foot as I edge down the slope. And the ground isn't loose dirt like the rest of the forest. It's like one giant rock, almost like the dirt has melted together from the heat of the crash. When I get closer to the meteor, I notice a faint blue light coming from deep within, shining through the cracks in the jagged structure. Something about this whole thing makes me feel uneasy.

As I finally get up close, I'm surprised to find that there's almost no heat coming off of it. In fact, it seems like it's getting colder the closer I get. And maybe it's just my eyes playing tricks on me, but the blue light inside seems to be getting brighter too.

Standing next to it is an odd sensation. Large parts of it jut out above me, casting shadows like the trees in the forest. I look closer at the surface. It looks way more like metal than a piece of rock. Although maybe a meteor could be metal too. I probably should've paid more attention in class. The air keeps getting colder as I reach out my hand toward the surface.

"There she is!" I hear from behind me. I whip around and see figures in bright green suits emerging from the tree line at the top of the crater. They found me again.

Maybe if I can get on top of the meteor, I can get away from them. I turn back and look up at it. I can totally climb that.

Quickly deciding, I reach up to start climbing the jagged surface. As my hand touches the cold metal there's a blinding flash of blue light from within, accompanied by a crack of noise, like lightning, that nearly blows out my eardrums. I close my eyes as I'm thrown backward. The air is knocked out of my lungs as I slam into the ground below.

I lay on the ground, trying to catch my breath, waiting for the ship's security officers to come pick me up. But no one comes. I open my eyes and slowly sit up. Both the meteor and the crater have completely vanished without a trace. The trees stand perfectly tall and unburnt around me. The entire forest biome is completely silent, save for the sounds of a couple songbirds high in the branches.

CHAPTER FOUR

THE MERCURY

I stand up and look around the grove but there's no sign of the meteor or any fires on the trees. They're standing as still and tall as they always have, no longer blown outwards from the crater. Something else feels different too but I can't quite put my finger on it. Oh, wait, all the alarms have stopped. They'd been going on so long I guess I just tuned them out. Although now without them the deck feels eerily quiet.

I glance up and there's no sign of any hole either. In fact, you'd never be able to tell that a meteor had just torn through it hours before. In the distance, I catch the shimmer of the bridleway stretching up above the trees to the next deck. Well, at least that's still there. My feet feel a little wobbly and it's hard to tell if it's from the new foot, being thrown backward by that weird pulse of light, or a combination of the two. I look around for my cane but can't seem to find it. Guess I'll have to find another somewhere. Without my cane, I do my best to stay stable as I find my way back.

The path looks the same as it did when I left, although this time other people are walking around. I get a couple of weird stares as I climb over the fence out of the wooded area, specifically from an older couple sitting on a nearby bench.

"Hey, what's everybody doing here?" I ask them.

They seem confused by the question. "What do you mean?" the first guy asks, his brow furrowed.

I look around at the other people out walking on the paths. Everyone is carefree and smiling. "The captain evacuated the deck!" I tell them.

"Did she?" the other guy asks, equally as confused as the first one. Something weird is going on here.

"You know what, I must've been confused." I decide to bail on this conversation after seeing the looks of utter confusion on their faces. Am I hallucinating or something? Did I just imagine that meteor hitting the ship? The path opens up into the courtyard around the bridleway. My new foot clinks against the tiled stones as I step off the dirt path and I can feel the cold stone against my other foot. Everyone's walking around here like nothing's changed at all.

I walk up to the entrance of the bridleway and blend in with the crowd. The entrance looks much nicer than usual. All the brass edges around the doorway look polished and new, which is something I haven't seen in years. Even the chariots inside look brand new. I wait on the deck with the rest of the crowd until one of the chariots pulls up in front of us, then follow the crowd inside. Some people grab onto the golden bars that hang down from the ceiling, but I slump into one of the velvet-covered seats around the edge of the pod.

The chariot starts to rise, giving me a spectacular view of the entire deck. No sign of the meteor anywhere below. Everything looks calm and still. The light from the deck filters in through the brightly-colored glass panels. I watch the colorful shadows move across the floor as we rise upwards. People around me talk about their days, what they want for dinner, their plans for the weekend, and everything seems pretty normal, which I guess is what's making me feel weird.

The chariot operator is wearing the same orange uniform they always wear, with that silly little hat, as he taps at the control panel in the middle of the room. The pod goes dark for a couple of seconds as we pass through the deck. I've always wondered what's between those areas. Maybe it's like what I found behind that secret panel on the Lido Deck. I honestly thought I had seen every inch of this ship but now I'm feeling like there's a lot more that I've never seen.

We gently slide into the station and I watch the crowd step out of the chariot into the plaza. I stay in my seat. This is the first chance I've had to sit down in what feels like forever. I rub where the metal of my new foot meets my skin softly since it's starting to feel sore. I think some of the other passengers noticed that I'm not wearing any shoes but luckily none of them mention it.

The doors close and the chariot rises up the bridleway again. The buildings on this deck stretch out far beyond the colorful windows, but just like the deck below, I can't see any sign of a meteor having crashed through. Maybe I really did imagine the whole thing.

"Deck Four," the operator says from his station, snapping me back to reality. I should get off here. I quickly get up and step out into the plaza around the bridleway. The bustle of hundreds of people around me feels different than it had before I found the meteor. Much less chaotic. This feels just like the regular business of the ship rather than people running around because a meteor just ripped through the hull.

The steps down from the plaza to the main streets look the same as always, kids running up and down them, people sitting and talking, and even someone playing an instrument for a small crowd. My foot echoes loudly off the cobblestone and I wobble every time the metal and stone meet. It definitely doesn't feel natural just yet. Also, now that I look closely at it, something about this street feels different, but I can't put my finger on exactly what it is.

I duck into one of the narrow alleyways off Main Street and follow it to a small courtyard. The marble statue in the courtyard's fountain has water flowing out of it loudly, masking the sounds of the crowds from the street over. I breathe deeply and take in the smell of the water and fresh flowers planted around the courtyard. Everything seems a bit cleaner than usual, and I can't even remember the last time they turned the fountains on. Maybe that's the change I'm noticing? But it feels weird that suddenly everyone would tidy up the ship and turn the fountains on while I was knocked out in the medical ward. That's a really elaborate and subtle practical joke to play on someone.

My quarters aren't too far away from here. Ok, I'll try heading back there to get my bearings and figure out what's going on. I pass under a stone archway out of the courtyard into another narrow alley. I run my hands along the walls as I walk, still a little uneasy on my foot and nervous about taking another tumble. Part of me wishes I still had that cane as I weave my way through the other people walking down the alley.

It's actually kind of weird that I haven't run into anyone I recognize this close to my quarters. Usually, by this point I've run into a couple of my neighbors, or at least someone whose face looks familiar. I follow the alleyways toward my quarters, passing under more stone archways and listening to the hum of all the floating planters.

I finally get back to my neighborhood and feel relief wash over me. At least being back home will help me feel better. I lean against the wall as I make my way up the stone steps toward my front door. I place my hand on the large panel next to the door and it buzzes loudly, flashing red.

"Unknown passenger. Please attempt identification again," a soft robotic voice says from the panel. That's weird, I've never had an issue with it recognizing my handprint before. I try again but the panel buzzes and flashes red again.

"Unknown passenger. Please attempt identification again," it repeats. I stare at my hand and look at the panel. What the hell is going on? I press the small bell icon on the panel and hear a loud chime from the other side of the door. At least the doorbell seems to be working. With any luck, my mom will be home and can let me in.

The door slides open and there's a girl about my age standing there. She looks so familiar, but what's she doing in my living quarters? "Can I help you?" she asks. She greets me with the same look of confusion on her face that I've been getting everywhere lately. And where do I know her voice from?

"I—" I can't seem to find any words to express what I'm feeling right now.

The look on her face shifts from confusion to concern. "Are you ok?"

"I must have the wrong place." I turn away.

"You sure you don't need anything?"

"Nope, just got turned around." I quickly start making my way back down the steps, away from my quarters. I hear the door close as I turn a corner into a nearby alleyway. My heart is beating quickly after that encounter, and whatever weird feeling I was having before just got multiplied by like a thousand.

By the time my heart stops beating out of my chest, I'm completely turned around. Probably should've paid more attention to where I was going. I step out of the alleyway into a small, enclosed garden and, luckily, I'm the only one here. I don't think I'm in the right headspace to interact with other people since my past few interactions have all been somewhat disastrous.

Underneath one of the large, blossoming trees, there's a simple stone bench which I walk over to. It's polished smooth, and despite being a little cold, it's still comfortable to sit on. I take a breath and try to calm down. I feel like I've just been running nonstop, and my foot is seriously hurting.

I take a closer look and see my ankle is red and swollen around where the metal's been rubbing against me. My other foot is also a little sore from putting all of my weight onto it. I can't seem to win with either right now. And since the ship doesn't actually seem to be in any immediate danger, I guess I can sit here a little while. My feet could use the rest.

There are lots of flowerbeds planted around this small garden, and a tall marble statue sits in the center of one, just like the one from the fountain in the other courtyard. Although that's not too surprising since they're practically everywhere on this ship.

Actually, this garden does feel familiar for some reason too. That's when it comes back to me like a wave. This was the same place I came to when I had a huge fight with my mom and tried to run away from home. I only made it as far as this garden before feel-

ing tired and hungry. But I do remember one of the gardeners sitting with me and sharing his lunch before walking me back home. He was old and super tall with worn-out overalls, but that's about all I remember of him. I wonder where he ended up.

I put my feet up on the bench and lay down, closing my eyes and listening to the hum of the floating planters. Now that I'm not being chased or dealing with the ship getting hit by a meteor, I can decompress a little. Plus, a garden with no other people around feels like the perfect place to hide out for a little while. I start to drift off.

✦

When I wake up, I feel groggy. My feet are a little better, but my neck is sore and stiff. My joints crack loudly as I pull myself up. Probably what I get for taking a nap on a stone bench. The courtyard is still mostly quiet, and the lights have dimmed.

Slowly, the lamps floating along the streets begin to turn on, humming just like the floating planters. Guess I must've slept for a while if it's almost night. Suddenly I remember the girl's face from my quarters and something clicks in my mind. She actually kind of looks like my mom. Maybe she's related to us somehow? But I don't remember my mom mentioning any other family, especially anyone my age.

I stand up and try to think about where to go next. As I do, my stomach growls. Well, I guess that decides it, then. I gotta find something to eat, otherwise I'm not going to last much longer. In fact, it's probably been almost a full day since I've eaten. Come to think of it, the last thing I ate was a few bites of that awful food in the brig.

I make my way down one of the alleys away from the garden and back towards the main road. The alley is dimly lit by the lampposts and very few people seem to be walking around here. Although when I get to the main road it's a little different; people are back out on the street here, ducking into houses and small shops along the way. Some of the cafes and restaurants in this quarter have tables set up outside where people are sitting and chatting.

There's still a very weird feeling about the ship. I still can't place my finger on what, but something is definitely weirding me out. Maybe I should find a safe space to hang out for a little while. I could head back over to the quarantined area. I doubt anyone will be looking for me over there.

I follow Main Street out of the residential area, take the bridleway down to the entertainment deck, and make my way to the quarantined area. For years I used to think that deck ended behind the coliseum, but I guess the ship still has a few secrets left to share. When I finally reach the wall, I follow it to the entrance I used to get into the Lido Deck before.

Much to my surprise, the entrance is no longer boarded up with large metal panels. Rather, the massive bulkhead doors are wide open, inviting people inside with a giant illuminated sign that reads 'LIDO DECK'. I step under the archway and the near-blinding light of the sign to find myself in the small cafeteria again.

The whole room feels completely different. First off, there's no massive hole ripped through the ceiling. Instead, there's a large mural painted over it, accented with gold that catches the light as I walk underneath. Second, all the random things that were floating around the room are now secured to the ground. The utensils rest on the tables where they belong, the potted plants sit firmly on the ground, and dozens of people sit around the tables eating meals together. But perhaps the weirdest thing is the cacophony coming from the opposite side of the room.

I'm drawn in by the loud noises and bright lights coming from the far bulkhead doors and move towards them slowly, trying not to bump into people as I shield my eyes from the light.

My jaw drops as I step out onto the deck. This once-abandoned area of the ship is bustling and full of life. The tiled floors are filled with sparkling pools of water and hundreds of people playing in them. More people sit beside the water in various deck chairs, chatting, playing, and just generally hanging out. Even the large white statues are painted bright colors and have water flowing out of them into the pools below. The entire deck is absolutely breathtaking.

There's a warm heat on my skin as I walk further in. I look up and see a series of bright red lamps shining down from the ceiling, obviously the source of all the heat. I wonder if those are the same kind they use in the biodomes. The bars are also filled with people in swimsuits with fancy drinks and large plates of food. Oh right, food. I still haven't eaten anything.

As I walk around in a daze, I'm startled by a loud mechanical voice from the box beside me. "Hi, I'm Chip! Can I interest you in a refreshment?" the vending machine says.

I roll my eyes but turn to face Chip anyways. "Oh, you again." While I do still hate AI, part of me is a little relieved to see a familiar face. As much as any AI can be a 'familiar face', I guess.

"I have a wide range of assorted snacks and drinks," it tells me.

"It's almost like you read my mind." I reach into my shirt, pull out my mom's old ID card, and tap it on the front of the machine. Hopefully, this will still work.

"Please make your selection." A small menu replaces Chip's artificial face on the screen. I scroll through, looking at the snacks available, wishing I wasn't so hungry and debating what would happen if I tried to buy everything at once. I tap on a small bag of pretzels and a drink to go with it. Chip's face reappears.

"Your refreshments will be available shortly." A small compartment opens up in the front of the machine and I watch as the pretzels and drink are placed gently inside by a small mechanical arm. I grab the snacks from the machine and the compartment door slides quietly shut.

"Enjoy!" Chip says loudly. I turn away and look for a spot to sit when something occurs to me.

"Wait, you have an AI unit, right?" I turn back towards Chip.

"That is correct! I've been programmed with the full range of hospitality services this ship can provide to our passengers," Chip responds in its chipper voice.

"Can I ask you some questions?" This vending machine might actually be more useful than I originally thought.

"You just did!" It takes every inch of my willpower not to smash this machine to pieces. This is why I can't stand AI units. They all have an unrelenting sense of 'humor'. I decide to push past it.

"Ok, I'm gonna assume that's a yes. First off, where am I?" I ask, opening up the bag of pretzels and shoving a couple in my mouth.

"You are currently on the Lido Deck! One of this ship's many venues of entertainment. You can find—"

"You can stop there," I cut it off. "And just to be sure, this is the *Mercury*?"

"Yes, you are currently aboard the starship *Mercury*. Current time 9:32PM, August 2, Ship year 0217."

That gets my full attention.

"Wait, what did you just say?"

"You are currently aboard—"

"No, not that part. What year did you say it was?"

"The current ship year is 0217."

My heart sinks. "Are you completely sure?"

There's a momentary pause before Chip responds. "Yes, I am fully synchronized with the ship's internal clock. The date I gave you is correct."

Twenty-one years. Somehow, I'm back twenty-one years in the past. That can't be possible, right? I sit down on a nearby bench and try to process this new information. My heart is beating out of my chest and I'm completely overwhelmed.

I open the drink from Chip and chug about half of it before pausing. The mango taste lingers in my throat as I look around the deck again. So that's why everything looks completely different here. But really, time travel? Feels like something out of one of the old reels from the library.

Wait, that means the girl from my quarters didn't just look like my mother, it probably was her from twenty years ago. That fact alone is a little too much for me right now. I eat some more pretzels and keep trying to piece everything together. I reach back into the pretzel bag and find it completely empty. Did I really eat them all already? The smells from the food over at the bar waft my way.

I follow the smell over to one of the seats at the bar. The people sitting around me all have elaborate-looking drinks with pieces of fruit stacked along the brims of their glasses. I've never seen uniforms like the ones the bartenders are wearing, pure white with light green trim. Mixed in with the human bartenders are a bunch of hospitality robots taking people's orders and offering drinks. I remember seeing a few of them off the last time I was here. One of the bartenders approaches me as I'm admiring his uniform.

"You need something?" He leans over the counter.

"What kind of food do you have here?"

He taps the table in front of me and a small screen appears on the surface. "Menu's right here. Just lemme know when you're ready to order." He smiles and walks back to the other people. I scroll through the food, but I have no idea what I want to order. Honestly, I've never even heard of most of these dishes. I smell something incredible and look up to see a large plate of food being given to a woman a couple of seats down by one of the robots.

The bartender walks back over to me with the same cherry smile. "You see anything you like?"

"What's that?" I point to the plate of food in front of the other woman.

He looks slightly puzzled but never drops the grin from his face. "Those are fries. You want some?"

I nod. "Yeah, bring me a lot please."

"Feeling hungry?" He laughs loudly.

"Starved," I tell him.

"No problem, just scan your ID and we'll be good to go." He places a small digital panel in front of me. I hesitate. My mom's ID worked for the vending machine, but would it work here too? I guess there's only one way to find out. I tap the ID against the panel and there's a soft ping. The grin disappears from the bartender's face for half a second before returning. If I hadn't been tracking his reaction so closely I probably would've missed it.

"Be right out with those fries for you," he says, and my worries melt away. Maybe I was just being paranoid. I didn't realize how stressful even simple things like getting food were going to be. I spin around on my stool to face the pool and watch the people playing. The energy here is unlike anything I've ever felt on the ship. It's so enthralling that I don't even notice the person walk up beside me.

"Excuse me," the person says. I turn towards them and see it's a tall woman wearing a green uniform. She looks me over. "Are you Helena?"

Crap. She used my mom's name. Probably from my mom's ID. "Yes," I lie.

"I'm gonna need you to come with me."

My heart sinks again. I have a feeling I'm not going to be getting that order of fries after all.

CHAPTER FIVE

UNFAMILIAR

Even though I've never been in this room before, it still has the odd, familiar feeling of being thrown into the Proscenium. It's lacking the paintings on the walls and is nowhere close to the same size, but I definitely have the same feeling in my gut of knowing I'm in deep trouble. Apart from the uncomfortable chair I've been left to sit on, there's nothing in here.

I keep expecting to see my mom walk through the door, begrudgingly bail me out, and put me on some boring ship assignment for a month like she always does to punish me. Although I guess technically she didn't the last time. Maybe this time I'll get something better than a stern hologram, like her actually showing up in person. There's a noise outside and I quickly turn to look. A small metal panel slides open on the door but it's not my mother's face that greets me this time. It's the same woman who interrupted my order of fries back on the Lido Deck.

"I'm going to open this door and you're going to come with me. Do you understand?" Her face is stern and unfriendly.

I nod and the panel slides shut with a metallic screech, followed by some loud bangs before the door swings outward. I stand up and follow her out of the small room and down a bland hallway with dozens of identical doors. What is this part of the ship? Could it be the actual brig? I didn't think we had one. I thought that's why my mom always threw me in the Proscenium instead.

"In here," the woman says, opening one of the doors and ushering me inside. The room is identical to the last one except for the addition of a table to go along with the chair. All the furniture in here must've been the handiwork of the guy who made the chair in the other room because it looks equally uncomfortable. My suspicions are confirmed the second I sit down; super uncomfortable again.

"Stay," she says, closing the door behind me. She actually reminds me a little of Harry from back in my time. Neither are the most chatty people in the world but for some reason I feel like they'd get along.

"Do you know why you're here?" a static voice asks, echoing through the small room.

I look around. "Who's there?"

"Just answer the question. Do you know why you're here?"

"Probably the same reason I always am," I say.

"What do you mean?" the voice asks and I quickly realize my mistake.

"Nothing, it's not important."

There's a long pause before the voice continues, "You have not been here before. In fact, according to our records, you don't seem to exist at all." I don't respond. "And on top of that, you were caught using one of the most convincing fake IDs we've ever seen. Apart from one glaring error," the voice says.

"Oh? And what was that?" I'll admit they've caught my interest a little.

"Well, it's the fact that you're using the identity of First Officer Inez," the voice explains.

"Oh," I say. I guess that old ID must've been from back when she was the first officer. Or rather, back now. Guess I never really thought about when it was from.

"Do you know how serious it is to forge documentation?" the voice asks.

"I mean—"

"Stop," another voice echoes through the room. "This isn't getting us anywhere," the new voice says. I hear the static of the speakers click off. Then the door to the room slowly opens.

A tall woman walks in and the room suddenly feels much quieter. Her shoes click against the metal floor, echoing loudly and adding to the absolutely terrifying air about her. She's wearing a white jumpsuit with a large cape hanging off of the back, and her silver hair is pinned atop her head, making her seem even taller than she already is. Despite her terrifying aura, there's something about her that seems oddly familiar, a feeling I've been experiencing with increasing frequency over the last couple of hours.

"My name is Cassandra." Her deep voice is calming. "Do you know who I am?"

"No," I tell her.

"I am the captain of this ship." And that's when I realize why she looks so familiar; I've seen pictures of her, covering almost every inch of our living quarters when I was a kid. She's my grandmother.

"Oh." I don't really know how to react to her.

"Oh indeed," she says. I think I was only around four or five when she passed away, so seeing her towering over me now feels like I'm looking at a ghost.

"Who are you?" She looks directly into my eyes and my heart starts to beat faster again.

"I'm Lucy."

Her eyes soften a little. "Lucy. Good. What were you doing down on the Lido Deck?"

"Oh, I just got a little lost on the way to my residence," I start.

She wrinkles her nose. "Lie," she says bluntly. All the softness disappears from her eyes. It's like she's looking right through me.

"I'm an orphan who doesn't have a home," I try.

"Lie." Her eyes seem to get more piercing every time she speaks.

"I'm part of the secret police and I'm on a classified mission to protect this ship."

"Not that either." She pauses, not once breaking eye contact with me. "I'm going to give you one more opportunity to tell me the truth." She steps closer and I consider my options before responding. Ah screw it, it's not like she's going to believe anything I say anyways.

"Well, if you really wanna know, I'm actually from the future." She doesn't break her gaze but her eyebrow raises slightly.

"Oh really?" I can't tell what she's thinking but I get this unnerving feeling that she can tell everything that I'm thinking. She couldn't be psychic, right?

"Yeah." I don't really know what else to say.

She takes a step backward and looks me over. "If you're from the future, how about you explain exactly how you got here," she says.

I think about it for a second. "I'm not really sure…"

Her mind seems to drift somewhere else momentarily as she watches me. "You know that's not super helpful."

"I mean, it's not the most helpful for me either," I respond. I feel like I'm under a microscope.

Her eyes lock with mine again. "I'm not entirely sure what to do with you, Lucy."

"How about some food?" I say, half-joking. I can tell from the look on her face that she doesn't seem to think it's as funny as I do.

She turns towards the other side of the room. "Helena!"

"Yeah?" I hear the same voice that spoke over the speaker before.

"Come in here." The door opens up and my mother walks in, just as I had seen her back at our quarters a few hours earlier. Or I guess a little different now. This time she's in a sleek white uniform similar to my grandmother's.

She looks at me and gives an awkward wave. "Hey."

"Hey," I respond with equal awkwardness.

"Lucy, this is my daughter Helena. She's the first officer on this ship and I'm putting you in her care for now." The captain turns to Helena. "Take her back to quarters and find a place for her." She then leans in and whispers something to Helena that I barely manage to catch. "And keep your eye on her."

Cassandra nods to me quickly before leaving the room and I'm left completely alone with my mother. Now that I'm a little calmer and less panicked about everything being different on the ship, I finally have a chance to look at her face. It's uncanny but it really is her, much younger but definitely my mom. I think it's the eyes that prove it.

"Do I have something on my face?" she asks. I suddenly realize how long I've been staring right at her.

"Ah no, sorry. You just look familiar."

"Well, you were at my quarters this morning," she says.

"Oh yeah, that must be it," I lie.

"Come with me." She makes for the door and I quickly follow her out, happy to be away from the most uncomfortable chair. We head back down the same hallway I had been brought up before, passing by all the random doors until we're near the top of the bridleway.

"So, am I, like, a prisoner?" I ask as one of the chariots slides up in front of us.

She stops in her tracks and turns to me. "Oh my god, what?"

"I heard what she said about keeping an eye on me," I explain.

"Oh, that." She rolls her eyes as the two of us step into the chariot and take a seat. I don't think I've ever seen her make that kind of expression before. "That's more about me than it is about you," she says.

"How so?"

"She wants me to do more, I guess. Get me ready to become the captain." She sounds less than enthused about it. The smile fades from her face as her mind appears to drift off.

"Don't you want to be the captain?"

"I'm not really sure. Doesn't feel like I've got much of a choice, though." She looks out the window, watching the scenery as we descend through the different decks. The chariot comes to a slow stop on the residential deck and we both get up without saying a word. She seems to be deep in thought.

"That's weird because you fit the role so well in my time," I try to assure her.

She seems to consider what I said for a few seconds before responding. "Are you really from the future?"

I laugh and give her a big smile. "Yeah, I am."

"Really?"

We make our way across the plaza towards Main Street. "Really."

I can still see the doubt on her face, no matter how much she tries to mask it. "And you have no idea how you got here, right?"

I smile but my heart sinks a little when she asks. "Not a clue."

"Huh." I can feel she doesn't buy it.

"You don't believe me?"

"I'm not really sure. Sounds kind of fantastical, if you ask me."

"Then why are you helping me? Is it just because the captain asked you to?"

She shakes her head but keeps walking. "Look, the captain can be kind of intense. You looked like you could use a friend," she says, and I smile. I wonder if she's ever been stuck in that same room with the captain.

We pass by a lot of people and I catch them staring at my mom as we walk by. She seems to ignore their stares, though. I actually kind of get how she feels. Back in my time, I'd catch people randomly starting. Guess that kind of comes with being the captain's daughter.

She looks me up and down. "Do you mind if I ask you another question?"

"Shoot."

"What the heck are you wearing?" I look down at my eclectic outfit, medical pants and shirt, leather jacket from that girl with the

bike, and no shoes. I guess I've been so focused on other things like time travel that I
completely forgot how ridiculous I must look.

"I've been a little busy. Haven't really
had time to change into anything else," I say.

"Oh, good. I was wondering if that's how
people were dressing in the future." We both
laugh and I can't remember a time when I've
laughed with her like this. Maybe sometime
when I was a kid, but no specific memories
come to mind. Nevertheless, for the first time
since getting stuck here, I'm almost at ease
again.

We arrive back at our quarters and I follow my mother up the stone stairs. I watch as
the panel pings and lights up green for her,
exactly like it didn't for me. Light pours out
of the doorway as it slides open and we step
inside.

I didn't get a good look the last time I
was here, but now that I'm inside everything
looks completely different from my time. I
can tell the overall structure is the same, but
almost all the decor is different. The furniture
matches the plain white walls, and all the old
paintings are gone.

"It's very clean," I say, trying to be nice.

"Oh, come on, it's so bland in here." She
takes off her shoes and kicks them onto a
small mat near the door.

"Ok yeah, why isn't there anything in here?" I laugh.

"It's my mom's choice. She did all the decor in here. Totally not my taste." We walk into the living room where the bland decor continues. Even the scenes on the windows seem dull, just random views of a plain landscape. She catches me looking at the scene and flips the switch next to the window, switching it to a beautiful recording of an ocean with the sun setting over it.

"I like this one better," I tell her. Back in my day, this was one of the regular views from the windows in here.

"Yeah, it's one of my favorites." She stares at it for a few more seconds before turning to me. "Ok, come see my room." She grabs my hand and tugs me down the hallway. But not to her room, to mine. She never told me she used to live in here.

Seeing the inside of her room, there's no doubt it's hers. It's a big difference from how the rest of the quarters are decorated. In fact, it looks just like how our quarters always looked back in my day. The furniture is old and cozy-looking, with lots of large knit blankets draped over the backs of the chairs.

The old paintings that usually hung out in the living room now coat the walls of this room and are hung so close together they're almost overlapping. It's like she tried to cram as many of them into this space as she possibly could. When they adorned the walls of our quarters, they always felt so manicured and uptight, but seeing them like this feels completely different. It actually kind of reminds me of my own room.

"I like this space a lot better," I tell her.

"Good, now we gotta find you something better to wear." She smiles and opens the closet, which is stuffed to the brim with clothes. She reaches in and pulls a few things off the rack, gently tossing them onto the bed.

"Are you sure this is ok?" I ask, looking over all the clothes.

"Oh yeah, you look ridiculous." She smiles at me for a second then we both start laughing.

"Come on, it's not my fault, ok?"

"Luckily we're pretty much the same size, so I think everything should fit you." She tosses a couple more options onto the bed. Weirdly enough, some of these are mine now, though they look a little more worn in my time. The doorbell rings and she stops pulling stuff out of the closet.

"Oh! I forgot to mention, some of my friends are coming over for dinner tonight. You'll like them." She rushes over to the door. "Once you find something to wear come join us and we can all have some dinner." She leaves and the door shuts behind her.

I start sorting through the small mountain
of clothes on her bed. She somehow managed
to pull out about half her wardrobe while we
were talking. I pull the leather jacket off my
shoulders and drop it over the back of a chair.
It's a little scratched up but all things considered, it's held up pretty well for how much
it's gone through.

I pick up a pair of striped, orange pants.
Not really my style. I toss them over to the
other side of the bed. As I do, something at
the bottom of the pile catches my eye. There's
a corner of a deep green fabric sticking out. I
can't really tell what it is, but I tug at the corner, eventually managing to free it from the
pile of clothes, and hold it up in front of me.
It's a jumpsuit. The fabric is coarse and
rough, but I absolutely love the style.

I take off the shirt and pants from the
medical ward and toss them onto the floor.
Then I pull the jumpsuit on and sure enough,
it's a perfect fit. I tighten the belt and look at
myself in the mirror. I can't believe I've never
worn something like this before since it suits
me so well. Just as soon as I think that, my
eye catches the leather jacket on the chair.
Oh, that's going to be perfect.

I pull the jacket on over the jumpsuit and
turn back to the mirror. This is absolutely my
new favorite outfit, and maybe with a little bit
of pleading Helena will let me keep it. Or if

she doesn't, I can just steal it out of her wardrobe when I get back to my time.

I hear other people as I leave the bedroom. I turn the corner into the living room and see Helena sitting across from someone new. He must be nearly twice my height and even sitting down he's absolutely massive. He'd probably be intimidating if not for the big, dopey grin across his face.

"Hey! You look awesome!" Helena says as she notices me. "Come sit down." She waves me over and I take a seat next to her on the couch. "This is my friend Egon."

I smile at him awkwardly. "Nice to meet you."

"Nice to meet you too, Lucy. Helena has been telling me all about you." His voice is deep and quiet. He reaches out a hand and I shake it. The height threw me a little bit but looking at his face he's clearly about the same age as me.

"Oh yeah?" I say, curious to hear what she's been saying about me.

"She tells me you're from the future? Is that true?" he asks. I can't believe she told him that.

My face turns a little red with embarrassment. "Uh, yeah." He's going to think I've totally lost my mind.

"That's cool," he says. The most chill reaction I've ever seen from someone. I wonder what it would take to faze him.

"Isn't it?" Helena chimes in. "Also, Egon brought us a bunch of food from the gardens for dinner. You two stay here and chat, I'm gonna go start prepping." She gets up and walks over to the kitchen, leaving Egon and me sitting awkwardly across the living room from each other.

"So, what do you like to do?" I start, trying to break the ice.

"I like plants," Egon responds. He's certainly not the chattiest guy I've met.

"Do you have a favorite?"

There's a long pause and he looks deep in thought. "Sunflower," he finally says.

"Good choice." Silence again. I can hear Helena chopping stuff in the kitchen as I let the awkwardness of this situation wash over the two of us.

The chime of the doorbell breaks the silence.

"I'll get that." I jump up from the seat and run over to the door. I tap the panel near the door and it slides open with a woosh. Three new people are standing in the doorway.

"Who're you?" one of them asks. She's shorter than the other two by a significant amount and wears a pair of big, round glasses. She has short black hair and dark brown eyes that stare intensely at me.

"I'm a friend of Helena's." I think that's the first time I've ever called her by her first name and it feels totally weird.

"Oh, well I'm Iris." The girl squeezes past me into the quarters, apparently bored of our conversation already.

"I'm Nao," the taller of the other two says. They have long braided hair and wear a long, patterned robe over their outfit.

"And I am Masumi. Nice to meet you," the other one says. Her voice is very soft, and she wears a similar robe to Nao but instead of long hair, her head is completely clean-shaven. I move aside and they step into the quarters. I let the door close and follow them back to the living room.

Iris is sitting next to Egon, already deep in conversation. As I get closer, she quickly turns her attention back to me. "Ok, Lucy, Egon has filled me in." She stares intensely at me through her thick glasses, then sits forward on her seat excitedly. "He says you're a time-traveler."

"Uh, yeah I guess so." I can't tell if she's making fun of me. Her face does look pretty excited now, but she didn't seem too interested in me before.

"Well, we're the Science Squad on this ship so you've come to the right people," she explains.

"I've never heard of the Science Squad," I tell her. I thought I was familiar with every division of the ship.

"That's probably because it's just what we call our friend group," Nao chimes in.

"Yeah, it's not anything official or anything," Masumi adds.

Iris waves her hand and shushes them. "Ok, fine, we may not be official but we're all really into science. That's why we're fascinated by you."

"Why would I fascinate you? I'm not the most science-y person," I explain.

"But you time-traveled!" Iris jumps up from her seat. "That's the fascinating part. I have to know everything." Her arms wave wildly as she speaks.

"I don't really know much about what happened," I start to explain. Helena comes back into the room, much to my relief.

"What about when you're from?" Iris smiles with glee when she asks this.

"I'm from 2710."

I can see her doing the math in her head. "So you're from twenty-one years in the future!"

"Come on, stop grilling her. We can talk about it more over dinner." Helena beckons

everyone over to the dining room where a
bunch of food has been stacked on the table.
She catches my arm as I walk by. "Hey, sorry
about Iris, she comes on a little strong but
she's really nice once you get to know her."
She gives me a warm smile.

I join the rest of the group at the table and
look at the food laid out. Everything smells
absolutely delicious and I start by grabbing a
bun, setting it on my plate. As I continue to
pile food onto my plate, I realize just how
hungry I am. I can't even think about how
many hours it's been since I've had food. Or
maybe even days at this point. I've completely lost track.

"So, time travel," Iris starts, her mouth
still half-full of food.

"Oh my god, could you be more
tactless?" Nao reprimands her.

Iris closes her mouth and quickly finishes
chewing. Then without missing a beat continues, "Ok so, time travel," she says. "Tell us
everything about how it happened."

I decide to give her the abbreviated version of the story. Seems like I've told it
dozens of times at this point. "Well, a meteor
hit the ship, I touched it, there was a blue
light, then I ended up here," I say.

"What kind of meteor?" Iris asks.

"No clue. I was a little distracted by the
ship getting hit and everything," I say, taking

a pause to stuff some more food in my mouth. I'm not even sure what I'm eating but it melts on my tongue.

Luckily Iris turns her attention to the others at the table, giving me more time to eat. "Thoughts on the meteor? Go," she says to them.

"Well, the meteor would have to be super dense, right? To go through the hull of the ship?" Nao says.

Iris nods. "Yes, good point."

"Unless it was going at warp speed," Masumi adds softly.

"Occam's Razor," Iris says.

"What's that mean?" I whisper to Helena. This whole conversation is going completely over my head.

"Basically means the simplest answer is usually true. So, in this case, it's probably more likely that the meteor was a dense material than it was going at warp speed," she explains.

"Ah, makes sense," I say.

Helena refills the drink in front of me with a smile. "This is usually how the dinners go. They pick a topic and debate the scientific principles until dessert. Seems tonight our topic is you."

And as if on cue, Iris turns her questioning back to me. "So, Lucy, this light you saw, where did it come from?"

"I guess it came from inside the meteor."
I think back to the crater and the meteor
again.

"Thoughts?" Iris asks. Helena gets up
from the table and heads to the kitchen.

"Ancient alien artifact," Egon says with a
completely straight face.

Iris turns to look at him, unamused. "Um,
maybe. Anyone else have ideas?"

She turns away from Egon but I catch his
gaze and he gives me a quick wink. Ok, Egon
might actually be kind of hilarious.

"Random wormhole?" Nao says.

"Could be. That part is a bit of a stumper,
honestly," Iris says as Helena returns with a
plate of cookies. The smell of them wafts
throughout the room.

She smiles at me as she sets the cookies
down on the table. "Dessert time!"

I bite into one of them and it melts in my
mouth. "What are these?"

"Peanut butter cookies," she says.

"Peanut butter?" I ask. There's a pause in
the room and everyone turns to look at me
like I just killed someone.

"Do you not know what peanut butter
is?" Helena asks. Much like the rest of the
group, there's a look of pure bewilderment on
her face.

"It's new to me. Is it exotic or
something?" I ask.

"Like peanut butter and jelly?" Iris says.

"I know jelly," I say.

The silence hangs, broken only by the sound of me eating another cookie. "A future without peanut butter sounds pretty grim if you ask me," Egon says.

"I can't wrap my head around that. You're like our age and you've never had peanut butter?" Iris asks.

"No, is that weird?"

"It's by far the most unrealistic thing I've heard tonight," Iris says.

"More than time travel?" I joke.

"But it's peanut butter!" Iris almost sounds distraught.

Thankfully Helena steps in to diffuse the situation. "Well, we'll have to send you back with some." She picks up the tray of cookies and brings them into the living room, something that would've been unheard of in my time. Food was not allowed in this room.

I sit in one of the chairs and grab another cookie from the tray. "So, what do all of you do?"

"I'm a mail carrier," Iris says, having finally moved past the peanut butter topic.

"Wait, like with those red uniforms?" I ask.

"God, they still haven't changed the uniform by your time?" Iris sounds upset but the rest of us laugh. Those mail uniforms are probably one of the least-flattering uniforms on the ship. Especially with the little hats that go with them.

"Do you like it?" I ask.

"Eh, it's ok. I like when I get to do repairs on the mail cart. That's what I really love." She kicks her feet up onto the coffee table and Helena promptly knocks them off. I guess some things haven't changed too much.

"I work in the ship's archives," Masumi says.

"She's an apprentice," Nao says.

"And what do you do?" Masumi turns to Nao.

"I'm a chef," Nao says.

"Assistant chef," Masumi adds.

"Oh, come on, I'm almost a full chef," Nao argues.

"They're siblings," Helena leans in and whispers to me, and I laugh. It's been a while since I've been a part of a group like this.

I realize Egon hasn't said much since dinner, so I turn to him. "And what about you, Egon?"

"Gardener," he says. I think back to our earlier conversation.

"Guess that's fitting if you like plants!"

"Yup." He gives me a big, goofy smile. He's certainly not much of a talker but he might be my favorite of the group.

"Hey, you should come meet us tomorrow," Iris says.

"Meet you?" I ask.

"Oh, that's right, I haven't even told you about our hideout yet!" Helena continues.

"You're gonna love it. Plus, you'll get to meet the last member of our group, Helena's boyfriend," Iris teases.

Helena's face turns bright red. Wait, her boyfriend? Does she mean my father?

"Come on, Iris. Stop embarrassing me," Helena says.

"Well, we should probably head out," Nao says. I look up at the clock on the wall and see just how late it's gotten. The group all stand up and start to say their goodbyes. I get a lot of hugs from them before they're out the door and it's just back to me and Helena again.

"I don't know about you but I'm absolutely exhausted," she says.

"Same, completely wiped out." After a giant meal like that, I feel like I could sleep for a week.

"I can imagine, you've had quite the day. Let's get some rest."

I follow her to our room where she rolls out a small mat on the ground. She ventures into her closet again and pulls out some extra pillows, blankets, and a set of pajamas. We get ourselves ready for bed and I lay down on the mat. It's not the most comfortable I've ever slept on, but at this point I'm way too tired to care.

And yet despite how tired I am, I can't seem to fall asleep. Iris's words keep echoing through my head about my mom's 'boyfriend'. She had to have been talking about my dad, right? And, more importantly, does this mean I might actually get the chance to meet him?

CHAPTER SIX

ATTICUS

I open my eyes to a familiar ceiling above me. For a second, it feels like everything must have been a dream, that I had imagined the whole time-travel thing. I stare at the ceiling for a few minutes, pretending that I'm back in my room, back in my time. But then Helena turns over in her bed and the illusion slips away.

I sit up and my joints crack loudly. Something about sleeping on a thin mat on the hard floor didn't seem to agree with my body. I look over at Helena; she's fast asleep, much more peaceful than I had been on the floor. But I guess this is her bedroom, after all.

I go to leave the room, but I nearly jump out of my skin as the door slides open and I see the captain standing in front of me. Was she just standing by the door waiting for me?

"Good, you're up. Come with me," she says. I follow her to the kitchen, feeling a little embarrassed that she's all put together and

I'm still in my pajamas. She gestures to the table and I sit down.

"Did you sleep well?" She pours a cup of something for each of us before joining me at the table. She sets one of the cups in front of me and I grab it.

"Uh, yeah. It was fine." The cup is warm in my hands, steam rising from it in the cool kitchen.

"Good. I thought Helena could help you get acclimated to the ship," she explains.

"Yeah, she was great," I assure her.

"Yes, well, I want to talk about you." She takes a sip of the drink and I do the same. It's hot and bitter and definitely not to my taste. I try, unsuccessfully, not to let the disgust show on my face.

"What about me? I already told you everything I know yesterday," I say.

She puts her cup down and leans forward. "Yes. However, that's not what's at issue here. We don't have any idea how time travel works, nor do we have the resources to research it."

"What does that mean for me?" A pit forms in my stomach. This is such a heavy conversation considering I just woke up.

"It means we have to act under the assumption that you'll be staying here. And like everyone on the ship, it means you'll be assigned a job," she explains.

"Oh." It finally starts to hit me — I might not ever be going home. I decide to push that thought down for now and try not to think about it.

"We've scheduled you for an aptitude test later this week to figure out what you're best suited for." She takes another sip of her drink.

"I don't get to pick?" I ask, but she shakes her head.

"No, these things are all decided by the ship's AI."

We sit in silence while I absorb this information. I think about what kinds of jobs I might get put into but nothing that comes to mind seems like anything I'd want to do. And it's not like I can step in as first officer since that job's already taken in this time. And even if I could, I'm not sure that's what I'd actually want to do.

"You two already up?" Helena walks into the room, her hair a complete mess, and that's when I notice something about her that I had entirely missed yesterday. Her trademark mechanical leg is gone.

I think about that for a second. No, not gone. That's still in her future, none of it has happened for her yet. I look down at my own mechanical foot and wonder how much of an adjustment it was for her. She doesn't really talk about it much but it's certainly distinctive hearing her metal leg clanging against the ground everywhere she walks. A little intimidating too.

"I caught Lucy for some morning tea before I head out." The captain gets up from the table and Helena takes her spot. I watch as she carefully cleans out her cup, dries it, and places it back into the cupboard. She doesn't say anything more before leaving the quarters.

"What were you two talking about?" Helena asks me the second the door closes behind the captain.

"She wants me to get a job," I say.

"God, she has the same conversation with me like four times a week." There's a pause before we both break out laughing. She really has a way of making a situation feel less tense.

"This stuff is awful, by the way." I gesture to my now cold drink on the table.

"Oh yeah, no idea where she got that stuff but it's not my taste either." She takes the cup from in front of me and brings it over to the sink, placing it gently at the bottom. She turns back to me. "Ok, let's get ready. I wanna bring you to our hideout," she says, pulling me toward the bedroom.

"What hideout?" I ask. I've never heard her mention a hideout back in my time.

"It's where all of us like to hang out. It's a secret part of the ship," she explains.

"Are you allowed there?"

"Oh, probably not. But it's never stopped us before. It's been quarantined for ages now," she says as we both get changed out of our pajamas. I put on the same outfit I wore the day before with the green jumpsuit. I could probably wear it every day of my life and still be happy about it.

Once we've both changed, we leave the quarters and make our way through the streets to the bridleway. We pass by crowds just starting their days, likely off to their various jobs. Everything feels so normal it's hard to remember that I'm not supposed to be here.

We get into one of the chariots and ride it down a couple of decks until it comes to a slow stop. Helena pulls me out into the plaza of Deck Six. I don't come down to this deck very often since there's not really much to do here. The entire deck is just full of old artifacts and museums, and replicas of old buildings from Earth that everyone's completely bored of by now.

"Let me guess; you took over one of these old buildings?" I look at the old structures around us.

She stops and gestures wildly at everything around us. "What? No! Our spot is way cooler than this old crap." She leads me down the twisting streets. A few people walk in the nearby fields, but apart from that the deck is deserted. We pass by more of the old structures, including a large marble building with dozens of columns. If I remember correctly, that one is the ship's archive. After about ten more minutes of walking, Helena finally stops in front of a large building with the word 'Observatory' etched into the stone above the door.

"So, we're going to the observatory?" I joke. I remember coming here on dozens of school trips.

"Come on, don't you trust that I'm bringing you somewhere cool?" she asks.

"Ok fine, show me what you got." Instead of walking up the large stone steps in front of us, she walks around to the back of the building. There's a large piece of fabric covering the ground which she pulls up, revealing a metal door.

"Help me get this open." We both pull at the door until it swings upward, landing on the ground with a loud clang. Thankfully no one seems to be around to notice any weird sounds. Inside is a small ladder.

"After you," she says. I look down into the hole and see nothing but darkness.

"You've got to be kidding me," I say.

"Funny, when we met you seemed like the adventurous type." She winks at me.

"Fine," I say, kneeling next to the hole. I lower one leg onto the first rung with no issue. However, as I swing my other leg down, I hear the metal of my foot clang against the ladder. This might be a little harder than I thought. I carefully lower myself into the hole, trying to keep all my weight on my good foot, but I feel the strain in my arms.

Climbing down takes a while, but eventually my foot connects with the ground. Helena climbs down much easier, taking only a couple of seconds at most.

"Ok, follow me." Without hesitation, she leads me down a small corridor. There's a light ahead of us coming from the end of the hallway and I can hear voices. We step out of the hallway into one of the most spectacular rooms I've ever seen in my life.

The room is absolutely massive, and in the center hangs an equally large metal globe with dozens of rings spinning around it. The whole structure floats in the air and, from what I can tell, doesn't seem to be connected to anything else in the room. Above the globe, the ceiling is painted with massive murals of stars, people, ships, and dozens of other scenes but it's tough to make out all the tiny details from down here.

The far wall is made from thick glass, just like the Lido deck, and built into the middle of the glass wall is something that looks like a large telescope with a platform attached and a winding metal staircase leading up to it.

There's someone up on the platform that I don't recognize, but before I can investigate I'm interrupted.

"Hey! You two made it!" Iris runs up to us.

"Hey, Iris, thought I'd bring Lucy around and show her what we've got here," Helena says.

"Let me give you the grand tour!" Iris says, tugging me away from Helena. She brings me to the far side of the room where Nao is sitting by a large computer console.

She pats Nao's shoulder but it doesn't seem to break their focus. "You've met Nao already. They're working on scanning the space around the ship."

"What kinds of things are you scanning for?" I lean in close and look at their screen.

"Planets, asteroids, really anything that's close enough," Nao says without looking up.

"But why?"

They shrug casually. "Mostly just for fun these days. See if we can find anything interesting out there."

"I mean, why would the ship even have scanning equipment like that?" I ask.

Iris chimes in with her thoughts, "My working theory is that they were looking for habitable planets to settle on. But when we found this part of the ship it looked like it had already been abandoned years ago, so it's hard to know for sure. And there are limited records on it all."

I look around the room again. Now that she mentions it, it does look like some parts haven't been touched in a long time. Iris pulls me along to another spot where Masumi is sitting in a weird, enclosed chair that looks kind of like a glass egg. Her eyes are closed and she's wearing a big set of headphones over her ears.

"What's she doing in there?" I whisper to Iris.

"She's listening," Iris says.

"Very helpful," I say sarcastically.

"Much like Nao, she's looking for anything interesting out there. Seeing if we can pick up some kind of signal with the ship's radio array," Iris says.

"Has she ever picked up any signals?" Masumi's face looks so peaceful, almost like she's asleep. In fact, if it weren't for her hand slowly rotating one of the dials on the control panel, I'd absolutely think she was asleep.

"Not yet, but that doesn't mean she won't!" Iris says.

"So, she's just looking at stuff like the asteroids and planets nearby, like Nao?" I look back out into the space beyond the giant glass wall.

"Ah no, the ship's radio array was designed to pick up signals from light-years away! Someone could send a signal from halfway across the galaxy and we'd still be able to pick it up here," she explains.

"Oh, ok. That's actually pretty cool," I say.

"Yes, it is cool," Iris says as she continues around the room. We get back to the large platform near the window and I see Helena standing up there next to the other person who suddenly spins around dramatically.

"WELCOME TO THE OBSERVATORY," he shouts, stretching his arms out wide. He's got wild hair, large glasses, and the most eclectic outfit I've ever seen. He's wearing a nice vest and trousers with a bow tie, but it's made infinitely sillier by the massive white lab coat that he's pulled on over the entire look, clearly not his size since the cuffs look like they've been rolled up pretty far.

"Oh stop." Helena pushes him playfully and I realize instantly who he is. He's my father.

"That's Atticus," Iris says as Atticus and Helena climb down the stairs toward us.

"Helena was just telling me about you!" Atticus says as he reaches the bottom of the stairs. He holds out his hand and gives me a firm handshake. For some reason, my brain can't seem to find the words to react to this. "I'm Atticus!" he says cheerfully.

Atticus. My father. When Iris mentioned my mom's boyfriend I wasn't sure if it would be him, but the second I saw his face I knew for sure. His hair is the exact same color as mine, just a lot messier. His eyes are the same hazel shade too. I can see why my mom always mentioned the resemblance between us. I find myself tracing over every inch of his face with my gaze, just taking him all in.

He's not that much taller than me either. Not sure why I expected him to be so much taller. He looks at me and my heart beats quicker. I thought I would know how to react but now that I'm here I don't actually have any idea how to behave. I always hoped to learn more about him, but I never dreamt that I'd ever get to meet him.

"I was just giving her a tour of the place," Iris chimes in, snapping me back to reality.

"Oh, well let me show you the coolest part of this whole place." He gestures to follow and I do, trailing behind him as he climbs back up the stairs. We reach the top of the platform and I see a seat with a large screen at the end of the telescope.

"What is this?" I finally manage to get some words out.

"It's the reason we call this place 'the observatory'." Atticus flips a switch and the screen in front of us turns on. "This telescope can see thousands of kilometers away from the ship." A bunch of stars appear on the screen.

"Where are all of these?" I ask.

Atticus points out the window towards a bright spot in space. "See that big cluster of stars? That's what the telescope is looking at."

I look back to the screen and see the same stars outlined before me. "What're you looking for out there?"

"Well, tomorrow night there's a large asteroid that's going to pass super close to the ship." I turn to him as he says this. It's hard not to get distracted looking at his face. After years of wondering what my dad was like, he's finally right here. It's bringing up a lot of strange emotions that I try to push down.

"Isn't that going to be dangerous?" I ask and he chuckles.

"No, we'll be perfectly safe out this way. It's going to pass close enough for us to see but shouldn't come any closer than a few kilometers from the ship. Plus, it's not like anything can damage the hull," Atticus explains. I think back to the hole in the ship back in my time and I'm not comforted. Whatever that meteor was made from was enough to rip a hole right through. Hopefully it's not the same one.

"Hey!" Helena calls up to us from below.

Atticus playfully leans over one of the railings. "Yes, my love?"

"Iris and I are going to run out for a little bit and grab us some food. Can you watch Lucy?" she asks.

"I can watch myself," I yell down to her.

"You're my responsibility while you're on this ship. And I'm putting Atticus in charge while I'm out," she yells back.

"I'll keep an eye on her!" he says before turning to me and giving me a big wink.

"Be back in a bit." Helena and Iris walk back out of the same hallway we arrived from.

Atticus turns to me. "So, time travel?"

"Oh, not you too!" I'm completely over talking about time travel with people.

"But it's fascinating to think about! Like, did you come through a wormhole? Or was it some kind of technology that got you here? Or could it have been aliens somehow? Or alien technology?" He keeps talking at a mile a minute.

"Look I have no idea how it actually happened, it just did." I can hear a bit of the frustration in my voice.

"I'm sorry, I can get a little carried away. I've just always been fascinated by science stuff like that. And if you're really from the future it means so much might be possible!" His eyes light up as he talks. It's still so weird seeing him like this. Before, the only idea I had of him was from an old photograph in my mom's quarters which he always looked so stoic in. But seeing him like this, he's so full of life, completely different than I had imagined.

"It's ok," I assure him.

"So, what do you want to talk about?" he asks and I see an opportunity.

"How long have you and Helena been together?" She never really talked about the two of them, so I guess this is my chance to pry a little bit.

Instantly his face lights up again with a big smile. "We've been serious for almost three years now. But we've known each other since we were kids."

"Wait, you knew each other as kids?" I'm already learning new stuff about them.

"Oh yeah, probably since like kindergarten. Then when we got our ship's postings after we graduated, I finally confessed to her," he says. I can tell he's reliving the moment as he tells me about it.

"That's sweet."

"She told me she knew all along. Guess I kind of wear my emotions on my sleeve, but we started seeing each other after that and have been going steady ever since," he says.

"That's really nice."

"Yeah, she's the best." He pauses. "So, tell me about yourself." I can see in his eyes that despite the casual nature of the question, he's clearly interested in talking about more serious things.

"Look, I'm really not in the mood to talk about time travel."

And almost like he can tell I knew what he was fishing for, he tries to play it off. "Oh no, I meant like what kinds of things are you into? Apart from the fact that you're a time-traveler Helena didn't really tell me much about you."

I think about it for a second. "I guess I haven't really told her much."

"So…?" He looks at me closely, clearly waiting for me to carry my half of the conversation.

"Oh, right. Well, what do you want to know?"

"Do you have any hobbies?"

Hobbies? I guess I haven't really thought about it too much. "I mean, I like to explore the different parts of the ship," I tell him, and I can see the excitement on his face.

"Really? Where have you gone?" he asks eagerly.

"Back in my time, the Lido Deck is fully shut down with no gravity, and I snuck in there," I tell him.

He looks shocked. "Wait, really? I've never heard of a part of the ship without gravity."

"Oh yeah, there were a bunch of plants floating around, even some vending machines drifting throughout the deck."

"I wonder why the gravity was off in that section," Atticus says.

"Well, the whole place had been quarantined. Actually got in a lot of trouble for sneaking in there," I explain.

"Ah yeah, I bet your parents weren't too happy with you breaking in, huh?" He jokes but something about that sentence hits me super hard. All at once the emotions I had been pushing down bubble to the surface. Like, how am I just sitting here having a normal conversation with my father? How do I break it to him that he's going to die? As various emotions suddenly well up inside me, I quickly stand up.

"I'm gonna run and grab some fresh air," I say, avoiding his gaze.

"Is everything ok?" He sounds concerned.

"Yeah, everything's fine," I lie and walk back towards the hallway. When I reach the ladder, I climb as quickly as I can. My breathing is short. I get a couple of rungs up before my metal foot slips and I fall onto my back. The wind is knocked out of me and I lie there for a second trying to catch my breath again.

"Damn foot." I slowly pull myself back up and try the ladder again, this time more careful of where to put my foot on each rung. I get to the top, push open the door, and emerge onto the main part of the deck. I have to get somewhere other than here.

My legs feel numb and my breath is short as I run toward one of the large open areas of the deck. My brain can't even think of where I'd want to go. Well, I know where I want to go. I want to go home. Back to my time. But that's not really an option, is it?

I'm nearby one of the other buildings on the deck so I keep running toward it. Tears slowly stream down my face, making it kind of hard to see anything. As I get closer to the building, I recognize it as the old gardens. Luckily there doesn't seem to be anyone else nearby which is perfect since I'm absolutely not in the right mindset to be around people right now.

I stop running as I pass through the iron gates to the garden. I walk up to the large hedges ahead of me and slowly step into the maze of plants. They tower above me on either side, and the smell of flowers calms me down a little. I still feel panicked, but this is helping. I follow the twists and turns of the maze until I come to a small open space with some benches and a fountain.

I take a seat on one of the benches and put my face in my hands. Tears roll down my cheeks as I let myself cry. I wish I was back with my mom again. Not Helena, but my actual mom. Even though we don't really get along it would be nice to see her again.

And even though I used to dream about getting to meet my father, this is nothing like I imagined it would be. I imagined sitting at a table with him, telling him about all the places I had explored, which is exactly what I was just doing, but for some reason the actual experience overwhelmed me.

I just wish I knew how I was going to get back to my own time. Everything here just feels so completely wrong and I just want to go home. I curl up on the bench and let the tears roll down my face as the lights of the deck dim into night mode.

CHAPTER SEVEN

THE PROSCENIUM

I have no idea how much time passed since I entered this maze, but judging by how dark it's gotten, it must have been a while. I think I cried all the tears in my body since my eyes feel dried out and my nose is runny. I'm sure to anyone passing by I look like a hot mess right now. Luckily, I seem to be the only one still in the gardens.

I look up at the deck far above me and see the stars shining, or at least the projections they put up there to mimic the stars. They don't compare to the real thing, though. I feel a little better but there's still a pit in my stomach. That uneasy feeling that I'm not going to make it back to my own time.

I hear a noise from nearby and look down to see Egon enter the clearing. He's carrying a random bundle of gardening equipment and looks just as surprised to see me here as I am to see him.

"What're you doing here?" I think that's the most words I've ever heard him say in a single sentence.

"What're you doing here?" I ask him.

"Gardening?" he says with a puzzled tone, holding up his bundle of tools.

"But why this late?"

He gestures to the flowers in the planter in front of us. "Because of these," he says. It just looks like a normal bed of blue flowers to me. Does he mean the statue in the middle of the flowers? But that would also be weird because those are everywhere on the ship.

"The flowers?" I ask.

"You mean you've never seen these ones before? Oh, you're in for a treat." And before I can explain to him that I've seen loads of flowers on the ship, he reaches down and runs his hand through them. As soon as his fingers come into contact with each flower, they begin to glow brightly.

"Wait, what the heck is happening?" I jump up from the bench and go look closely at the glowing flowers.

"They're bioluminescent," Egon explains.

"How're they doing that?" I reach out and touch one of the flowers. Just like what happened with Egon, as my fingers brush up against it the flower glows bright blue. I pull my hand away and notice a residue glowing on my palm.

"That's what I'm studying. My friends have their engineering and physics, but I happen to think the botany on this ship is way more interesting," he explains.

"But why do they glow?" I ask.

"No one really knows. My guess is that it's got something to do with the environment. Historically there's nothing about these types of flowers being bioluminescent." He gently picks one from the planter and places it into a small container before tucking it into one of the large pockets on his overalls.

"What does that mean?" I ask.

"It's got to be something about the ship. Is it the ship that's turning them bioluminescent?" he asks.

"Not a clue," I respond. He looks at me and from his expression, I realize his question was probably hypothetical.

Then I see another look come across his face — concern. "Are you ok?"

"Oh, yeah I'm fine," I lie.

"You look a mess," he says.

"Wow, you don't pull punches, do you?" I try to joke.

"I do not," he says, and I sit down on the bench again.

"I don't know, just being here is so much, you know?"

He places his gardening supplies gently onto the ground before joining me on the bench. "What's getting to you?" He sounds so sincere.

"I'm stuck here," I say.

He puts his hand on my shoulder. "That is tough."

"And I just met Atticus." That whole interaction felt like a mess.

Egon gives a little smile. "He can be a bit intense."

"It's not just that." I pause, debating whether to tell Egon the full story. His presence feels so calming I decide to be honest. "He's my father," I say.

"I don't understand." I can't bring myself to look at him directly but even still I can feel his gaze on me.

"And Helena is my mother." It actually feels good to tell someone about this.

"How is that possible?" He sounds completely taken aback.

"It's that whole time travel thing," I joke.

Egon pauses before responding. "I can see why you might be stressed about that."

"Yeah, I'll be honest, I've got no idea what to do about anything," I say.

"I'm sure the others would be willing to try and help you find a way to get back to your own time."

"I'm not even sure it's possible," I say.

"Usually I would agree with you but… you're here, right?" I think about that for a second. I mean, maybe there is some way to reverse what happened.

"I guess." I'm still not one hundred percent sure, though.

"If you got sent back in time, logically there is a way to send you back. We just have to find it." I lean in and give him a big hug. His clothes are covered in dirt but contrasting that is the strong smell of flowers that wafts around him. I hadn't really noticed it until now, but it's nice. He smells like what I imagine sticking my head into a flowerpot would smell like.

"Thanks for being so nice," I say.

"How about we get you back to the others? They're probably wondering where you got off to," he reminds me. We get up and begin heading back to the observatory. As we get to the exit of the garden, he stops me. "We're going to head back a different way," he says. "It's a little longer but an easier trip."

"Easier?" I ask.

He glances down at my metal foot with a knowing look. "There's no ladder to climb down this way."

"Oh…yeah, that does sound better." Falling off the ladder is certainly not a sensation I'm eager to repeat anytime soon. I nod and Egon leads us in a different direction until we reach a small hill in the landscape.

"Here." He leads me around the corner and I see a small cave on the other side.

"It's a cave," I say.

"It's the other entrance," Egon corrects me. He steps into the cave and pulls out the container with the flower he picked earlier. The blue glow lights up the space ahead of us, seeming to get even brighter the darker it becomes. I follow closely behind him as he leads us deep into the caves. Although I quickly realize that past the entrance it's just a normal ship tunnel. Same metal walls as everywhere else.

"Can I ask you a favor?" I ask as we walk through the darkness.

"Sure," he responds.

"Please don't tell Helena and Atticus about what I told you."

"I will not tell them," he responds. We walk a little further in silence.

There's something else that's been gnawing at me. "There's something about you that feels really familiar."

"Familiar?" he asks.

I can start to see a light glowing ahead of us. "Yeah, we haven't met before, right?" I try to think but my brain is tired. In fact, my whole body feels exhausted.

"You would know better than me," he says.

"I guess so. I've just got the weirdest sense of deja vu."

"We're back." We step into the observatory through an upper level. I don't think I even noticed this little balcony the last time I was in here. It looks down over all the various stations in the observatory.

"Where have you been?" Helena's voice rings through the room in a familiar way. For the first time since getting here, she sounds like my mom. She quickly runs up the stairs to meet us on the platform.

"I—" I start to say but Egon interrupts me.

"Lucy and I were getting some fresh air out in the gardens. Sorry to keep her so long."

Helena stops in her tracks. She looks at my face and her whole expression changes. "Are you ok? You look like you've been crying," she says.

Egon puts his hand on my shoulder. "I think it's just been an eventful day for everyone. Maybe a show would lift everyone's spirits," he says knowingly to Helena.

I finally manage to find my words again. "What kind of show?"

"One of the shows down at the Proscenium." I can hear how excited Helena is at the prospect.

"But it's all run-down…" And as soon as I say that I realize… "It's still open?"

"Wait, you mean to tell me you've never seen a show there before?" She looks completely shocked.

"Nah, they shut it down when I was little. I've only seen it abandoned." I decide to leave out the part about them using it as the ship's brig. This doesn't feel like the right moment for that.

"Ok, then it's decided. We're going to a show tonight." She grabs my hand and pulls me back down the tunnel Egon and I had just come from. Egon waves and gives me a little smile.

"Why're you in such a rush?" I stumble a little as she pulls me along.

"We've only got like two hours until the show and we've got to change and get ready." We reach the end of the tunnel and keep running back toward the bridleway.

"Why do we need to change?" I ask.

She looks me up and down quickly. "Because you can't wear a jumpsuit to a show at the Proscenium. It's a formal event," she explains. I find myself struggling to match her pace.

"The only formal event I've ever been to was the ship's anniversary gala when I was a kid. And that was super boring," I say as we reach the bridleway.

"Oh, this is nothing like those stuffy galas," she says as we step onto one of the chariots. It rises through the decks and the flickering lights from outside shine through the multicolored windows of the chariot like hundreds of rainbow stars.

It slides to a silent stop at our deck and we both walk out. The plaza is dimly illuminated by the lanterns floating along it, gently bobbing up and down, casting long shadows all along the cobblestone. Helena continues pulling me back towards our quarters. We turn down the familiar dark alleys until we finally reach the door.

"Come on, we've got to hurry." She pulls me inside and runs down the hallway to her room, with me steps behind. As I enter the room, she's already thrown open the closet doors and is frantically rummaging through all the hanging garments. She pulls out a beautiful blue gown with intricate white beading and sequins covering the length of it. She looks at it closely before tossing it onto the bed.

"Is that what I'm wearing?" I ask.

"Ah no, that one's for me. I was thinking about it on the way back. I still gotta find a good one for you." She continues to dig around in her closet. I'm a little relieved since that dress is pretty but definitely not my style. She pulls a pink silk gown out and holds it up in front of me before shaking her head.

"Nah that's not you either." She looks for a few more seconds before excitedly pulling one out of the rack of clothes. "I found the perfect one for you." She's got it hidden behind her back.

"Well, show me!"

She pulls the dress out from behind her back and holds it up. It's a lot less flashy than hers so I already like it better. The dress is a light cream color with small, colorful embroidered flowers along the bottom. I reach out and grab it from her. The fabric is soft, almost like cotton.

"It feels nice." I hold the dress in my hands and look up to see a big smile on Helena's face.

"I knew I'd find the perfect one for you," she says.

I walk over to the bathroom and let my hair down before tugging off the jumpsuit and letting it fall to the floor. I catch my reflection in the mirror and notice how much of a mess I look right now. There are dark bags under my eyes from all that crying. I turn the shower to hot and let the steam fill the room. Then I close my eyes and step into the stream of water, letting it run over me. My whole body relaxes and no part of me wants to be anywhere but here right now.

I wash the dirt off my foot, probably still there from running around the deck with no shoes on. I listen to the water hit the metal of my other foot, making a plinking noise with each drop. By the time I step out of the shower, I feel like a completely different person. All the grime of the past few days has been washed away, along with that looming feeling of despair that I was feeling back in the observatory. I change into the new dress Helena had given me and head back into the bedroom.

"Wow, it looks great on you!" Helena says. She's wearing the dress she picked out for herself, and her hair has been pulled back into fancy braids. "Come over here." She waves me over and I take a seat in front of her.

"What're you doing?" I ask.

"I'm doing your hair." She pulls my hair back and starts to weave it into thick braids along the sides of my head before tying each braid off. Her hands work quickly. I can't even remember the last time someone did my hair, certainly never her. Even for the ship's galas, she'd always bring in someone else to do my hair. After all, her work came first. And on my own, I'd usually just end up with it in a messy ponytail, completely untamed. I was never really one for doing my hair.

"There, we match now," she says after a couple of minutes. I stand up and look in the large mirror and I barely recognize myself.

With the new dress and hairstyle, I look like a different person. Helena stands next to me; our braids match almost exactly.

"Thanks for this, I feel a lot better," I say.

"Oh, just you wait, you haven't even seen the show yet." She sounds so excited. "And we should probably get going if we want to make it on time." She very quickly but gently starts pushing me towards the door. We rush out of the quarters together and run through the alleys toward Main Street.

We get there and, like most evenings, the street is brightly lit by the floating lanterns while people sit crowded around tiny tables in front of the cafes and restaurants, making loud conversation. As we run past, I catch glimpses of dozens of faces that look vaguely familiar.

In almost no time we're back at the bridleway, riding one of the chariots down. We arrive at the deck and follow the streets in the direction of the Proscenium. Back in my time, this whole part of the ship was completely run-down, but now it feels vibrant and full of life. All the venues are open again and lanterns float along the streets.

But perhaps the most impressive thing on this street sits right at the end. The front of the Proscenium towers above everything and its giant marquee sign casts a bright light over the top of all the other buildings for blocks.

The sign, which I remember being burned out with shattered light bulbs, is back to its former glory.

Helena catches me staring at the building. "Impressive, isn't it?"

"I've just never seen it like this." I'm in complete awe of how vibrant it looks. My eyes drift down to the large crowd gathered in front. Everyone is wearing outfits that are just as fancy as the ones Helena and I have on. It feels like one of the old galas but way less stuffy. We join the crowd and make our way toward the Proscenium.

The doors are ornate and carved with beautiful scenes that I can barely make out before we're past them and inside the main lobby. Giant crystal light fixtures hang down from the ceiling, lighting up the room. The floor is covered with a plush red carpet that my feet sink into.

"It looks so different," I say as Helena and I climb the grand staircase.

"What's it like in your time?" she asks. I look around and take in the entire room.

"Not a thing like this. It's all boarded up and covered in a layer of dust," I explain.

She looks a little sad. "Wow, I can't even imagine this place like that."

"Yeah, well I never would've imagined it like this," I joke. We arrive at the top of the staircase and enter through the doors into the main room of the Proscenium.

It's definitely the same room I always got thrown into whenever I was in trouble, although this time there's a noticeable lack of pianos. There's also no dust over the seats, the marble columns are all still in one piece, and the old paintings on the walls are no longer cracked and peeling away. I can finally make out some of the details in the older paintings from across the room.

Helena leads us down the aisle and we take our seats near the front as the rest of the crowd files in. I can't stop myself from looking at all of the details throughout the room. Although I do avoid looking at where the air vent is in the corner, not quite ready to relive any memories of that right now. Instead, I focus on the beauty of the rest of the room. In my entire time on this ship, I don't think I've seen anything quite this stunning.

"I can see why you like this place," I say to Helena.

She laughs. "Oh, the building has nothing to do with it."

"Then why do you like it here?" I ask.

"Well, it's my dream to be a singer someday," she says.

"Wait, really?" That's a complete shock. I've never once heard her mention anything about singing.

"Hey, it's not so silly! I'm actually pretty good at it," she protests.

"Why don't you do it, then?" I ask.

"Because I'm the captain's daughter. Everyone expects me to take over running the ship after my mom," she says. Now that's a feeling I can relate to, probably more than she'll ever realize.

"But what about what you want?" I ask.

"It's not really up to me," she says, but I can see that it hurts her to say that.

"But it's your dream!" I say, slightly too loud. A few people turn their heads disapprovingly towards us.

"It's just a fantasy. Maybe in another lifetime it could've been," she says. I'm about to keep talking but the lights dim and Helena raises a finger to her lips, giving me a soft shush.

The room falls silent as the lights fade completely out. I can feel the anticipation building as everyone waits for something to happen.

Suddenly there's a bright swirl of color on the stage, followed by another. The colors dance around the room, casting vibrant light over people's faces. They circle the room before ending back on stage. As the lights settle, they surround a group of four people. Three of them hold large instruments and the fourth steps forward to a small microphone.

As she does, the three people behind her begin to play, their music filling the room, bouncing and echoing perfectly off the walls. Her gown sparkles in the lights of the stage, seeming to shift between colors. It's hard to tell if it's the dress itself or the colors swirling around the stage. She opens her mouth and begins to sing.

Her voice is unlike anything I've heard before. It's loud but not in a bad way. It's so smooth I can feel myself relaxing as she sings. I'm so used to hearing music through recordings and speakers that there's something so pure about having the actual person in front of you.

The colors that were swirling around the stage begin to form into large shapes that float about us. The shapes solidify into hundreds of colorful flowers and I reach my hand out to touch one that's floating nearby, but my hand passes right through it. Wait, these are all holograms? I guess that makes a lot of sense, I've just never seen holograms used like this. Usually they're for ship communication. Or dramatic mothers.

I look over at Helena and notice her lips moving along with the song, not singing, just mouthing the words. Doubly impressive considering all the lyrics are in a language I've never heard before. She must've heard this song hundreds of times to know it that well.

But considering how beautiful this performance is I can hardly blame her for coming to see it so many times.

The show continues for another hour, sometimes with singing, other times just the instruments, but all the while with holographic images floating throughout the room. It's like being transported to another world. When the music finally stops and the holograms disappear there's a pause before the audience erupts into thunderous applause. Helena and I both stand up and clap along with the rest of the crowd.

"Wasn't that the best thing you've ever seen?" she leans in and says to me over the roar of the applause.

"I've really never seen anything close to that." I watch the singer and musicians up on the stage take a bow before leaving.

"Don't you think it would be cool to do something like that one day?" she asks.

"I'm not sure it would be my thing. I think I'll leave the performing to you," I joke. Honestly, the thought of being up in front of a crowd like that kind of terrifies me.

"I absolutely love it," she says. Guess that's still true about her, then. She was always pretty good with large crowds. Kind of comes with the territory of being captain. We start filing out of the theatre with the rest of the crowd.

"Hey, thanks for tonight," I say as we walk back down the staircase toward the lobby.

"Of course! I can't believe you've never seen a show here before!"

"No, not about that." She looks confused. "I mean not just for that. I was just… not feeling so great about everything," I explain.

She stops on the steps. "Are you doing ok?" The crowd continues to walk around us.

"I am now. Between venting to Egon and coming out to this, I'm in a much better mood," I say.

"Oh yeah, he's great to talk to," she says.

"He really is."

"Do you mind me asking what was getting to you?"

"Mostly the whole being-out-of-my-own-time thing," I say.

"And that's it?" She looks at me intensely and I think about the other things I confessed to Egon.

"Yeah, that's it." Which isn't really true but I'm not nearly in the right mindset for that conversation.

"Well, if you ever need to talk I'm here too," she says. We keep walking down the steps towards the lobby and make our way out of the Proscenium.

As we're walking along the street with all the other people in their fancy outfits a thought occurs to me. "Hey, what're you doing tomorrow night?" I ask, remembering what Atticus mentioned about the meteor that was going to be passing by the ship.

"Atticus and I are going to watch the meteor from the observatory." She smiles a little when she says his name.

"Well, if you're up for it, I know a much better place we could watch from," I say.

"Really?" She seems super excited about it.

"Oh yeah, but you're ok sneaking out, right?" I ask and she smiles.

"Of course I am. I sneak out all the time." Wow. I guess we are pretty similar.

"Good, we can bring Atticus too. I promise it'll be just as unforgettable as tonight."

I think I've found the perfect way to thank her for helping to cheer me up. And with any luck, we'll get a close-up view of that meteor.

CHAPTER EIGHT

SPACEWALK

Helena's alarm clock goes off and I stir awake, rolling over and hitting it quickly to turn off the sound. She said it wouldn't be that loud but it was definitely loud enough to wake the dead, or worse, the captain. Luckily it doesn't seem like it woke anyone else up, least of all Helena.

I shake her in a not-so-gentle attempt to get her up. "Hey, it's time for us to go."

"I don't wanna," she says, rolling away from me in her bed. I get up and turn on the lights. It's blinding but seems to do the trick. She sits up and looks at me with a dreary expression.

"We have to get ready," I tell her.

"It's the middle of the night." She yawns and stretches her arms above her head.

"Yeah, that's the whole point," I remind her.

"I just want to sleep," she protests. Her eyes are barely staying open.

"We're supposed to meet Atticus in a couple of minutes," I say. Finally, I find the thing that perks her up a bit. Her eyes open wide.

"Oh right, he's expecting us." She pulls herself out of bed and we get ready together, taking extra caution to make as little noise as possible. We don't want this adventure ruined before it's even started.

"You ready?" I ask once we've gotten ourselves together.

"Lead the way," she says, still clearly a little asleep. I gently slide open the door to her room and we sneak down the hallway towards the living room, shoes in hand to stay quiet. Although, while that may have been a good idea in theory, my metal foot clinking loudly against the ground has quickly proved otherwise. I try to tread lightly but each clink is almost comically noisy.

We finally reach the door to the quarters and it slides open. We exit and the door shuts behind us. Helena and I both let out a big sigh of relief now that we've cleared the first hurdle of sneaking out. We pull our shoes on and walk down the stone steps toward Main Street.

The lanterns are still bobbing brightly, however the crowds have disappeared, leaving the street completely empty. Most people are probably sound asleep at this hour. Not really the best time for socializing since, with the cafes closed, there wouldn't be much to do here anyways.

We walk along the empty street together until we reach the bridleway. We take a seat at one of the benches in the plaza and wait for a chariot to arrive. There's a lot less of them at night so we might be here for a bit.

"You still haven't told me where you're taking me," Helena says. With all the walking and the brisk night air, she seems to have woken up a little more.

"It's a surprise."

"Can't I even get a hint?" she asks.

"I'm just going to say it's probably the best possible place to see that meteor from," I tell her.

I can see her going over all the locations of the ship in her mind. "Is it the Lido Deck?"

"Why would it be the Lido Deck?" I ask.

"Well, it's got all those windows! Thought it might be good to watch stuff through," she explains. And I've got to admit, it's pretty solid logic. Even if it is ultimately wrong.

"Good guess, but no." I smile.

After a couple of minutes, a chariot finally pulls up to the station and we get up. Apart from the operator, who nods to us as we enter, there's no one else inside. We take seats facing each other on opposite sides of the pod.

"You two are up pretty late," the operator says, making casual conversation.

"Yeah, we're going to watch a meteor pass by the ship," I say.

"Sounds fun," she says, continuing to press various buttons in front of her. The chariot stops a couple of decks down and we both leave, nodding to the operator as we step out into another plaza.

I look around and notice Atticus standing a couple of feet away. Helena runs over and gives him a big hug, catching him off guard.

He turns around and gives her a big hug back. "Hey, you."

"You been waiting long?" Helena asks.

"Just a little while." He smiles at her and doesn't break eye contact. "So where are we off to tonight?"

"No idea, Lucy's been keeping it all a big secret from me." She nods in my direction. Atticus looks over and finally seems to notice that I'm there too.

"Oh, hey there, Lucy." He pulls away from Helena, looking almost a little embarrassed. His face is bright red.

"Hey, Atticus."

"Where are you taking us tonight?" he asks. His outfit is a lot more casual than the day before. If I didn't know any better, I'd almost say it was something he'd wear for a date.

"We're going to go watch the meteor together," I say.

"Yeah, Helena told me that much already.
But where are we going to watch from?" He
has this funny way of asking questions. Like
super casual yet somehow you could tell he
was holding back his excitement about the
answer.

"That's a surprise," I tell him.

"I can't imagine any place that would be
better than the observatory with our
telescope," he says.

"Oh trust me, this will be a much better
view than that," I say with a smile. I really
can't wait to see the looks on their faces when
they see where we're going. It's totally going
to blow their minds.

"Ok, lead the way, then!" Atticus says,
grabbing Helena's hand.

I lead them down one of the side streets
towards the edge of the ship. I've never liked
this part of the ship but sadly it's the only way
to get where we're going. It always feels like
they never actually finished building this section. Like instead of the nice cobblestone
roads they used on the other decks, they just
left the ground here unfinished metal.

Most of the buildings are nothing more
than frames. I've asked about it but no one
seems to know anything about this part. Although I've often felt like there must be at

least one person who knows. We come up on a massive building that sits right up against the wall of the ship. It's unique in that it's the only finished building we've come across.

"I didn't think there was anything down in this section," Helena says.

"Yeah, there's not much on this deck, but there is one cool thing." I stop in front of the building once we're close. The only sources of light on the entire street come from a small streetlamp in front of us and the dim light from the artificial stars on the deck above us. On the front of the building is a large metal door.

Helena starts to walk toward the building but I grab her and pull her behind a half-finished wall. "Hide," I whisper as Atticus ducks down with us.

"What—" Helena starts to say.

"Shhhh," I cut her off and hold a finger up to my mouth.

We crouch down in silence, watching the building until a figure comes out from around the corner wearing the unmistakable green security uniform.

"Why's there security down here?" Helena asks.

"Yeah, that does seem pretty odd," Atticus chimes in softly.

"We just have to wait for him to walk away," I say.

"Wait, we're going in there?" Helena asks.

I smile. "We absolutely are."

"Aren't you going to tell us what it is?" Atticus asks.

"Nope, that's still part of the surprise." I smile even wider. We wait silently for the security officer to round the corner again and then quickly bolt towards the door, now fully out in the open with the streetlight shining down on us. I give the door a big tug and it swings open. I pull it closed behind us once we're safely inside.

Neither Atticus nor Helena say anything as they walk further into the room. Even through the dim light in here, I can see the awe on their faces as they take in the giant structures in front of them.

"What is this place?" Helena finally breaks the silence. Her eyes are locked on the massive object directly ahead of her.

"It's an old shuttle bay," I explain.

"A what?"

Atticus walks up to one of the shuttles and runs his hand along the side. "So this is where the shuttles were kept." It's about three times his height and made from a dark black metal that seems to shimmer as we walk past it.

"Wait, you knew about the shuttles?" Helena asks.

"Yeah, back in the observatory there were a bunch of old records of them," he explains.

"What kinds of records?" I ask.

"Well, a lot of the old equipment in the observatory was for surveying planets and other things we found out in space." They both seem a little distracted by the massive shuttles. "There were records of actual manned surveys from very early in the ship's journey. But I had just assumed all of the shuttles were destroyed over the years. Or stripped for parts." I can see the gears turning in his head as he takes everything in.

"Nope, they've been sitting right here the whole time. Although back in my time there's one less shuttle so maybe they did start taking them apart for parts. Guess they're not doing much good just sitting down here in storage," I say.

"I wonder if they're still working," Helena says.

"It would be worth checking. Heck, I'm sure with the whole team we could probably get one up and running again." Atticus sounds practically giddy before a look of realization appears on his face and he turns to me. "Wait, don't tell me you plan for us to watch the meteor from one of these old things?"

"Oh, definitely not." I laugh. "I'm not crazy enough to try and fly one of these on my own. I'd probably end up crashing it into something."

"Then why did you bring us down here?" Helena asks.

I point over at a series of lockers on the wall. "Because we need spacesuits"

"Spacesuits?" Helena looks confused.

"Ok, I'll finally tell you, we're going to watch the meteor from the outside of the ship." I smile widely.

"WHAT?" both Helena and Atticus exclaim.

"Oh, come on, it'll be fun!"

"How would we even get out there?" Helena asks.

I walk over to the lockers and pull one open, showing off the spacesuit and helmet inside. "There's a small airlock a deck up that we can use."

"But wouldn't that be dangerous?" Helena asks.

"I've done it dozens of times! It's totally safe," I explain. Helena looks nervous but Atticus is staring intensely at the spacesuits.

"It would be a great spot to see the meteors from…" he starts to say. I can already tell he's hooked.

Helena rounds on him. "You can't be serious!"

"Just think about it! You and me, walking on the side of the ship. Now how many people can say they've done something like that before?" He smiles at her for a few seconds before she finally gives in.

"Ok, you do make a good point."

"Perfect!" I grab the first spacesuit out of the locker and hand it to Helena. She holds it up in front of her while I open the rest of the lockers and search for two more suits for Atticus and myself.

"Lead the way," Atticus says. The three of us sneak back out of the shuttle bay with the spacesuits in hand and quickly make our way up to the next deck.

Tucked away in the far corner of the deck is a small door with a painted red wheel mounted to the middle. I've been through this door more times than I can count, but to any passerby it probably looks like every other maintenance closet.

I pull on the wheel, the metal screeching as it turns slowly. It spins a little quicker than I'm used to with Atticus and Helena helping. The wheel finally stops and the three of us tug on the door together.

"The door is so thick," Helena says as it slams open.

"That makes sense if it's part of the airlock," Atticus says. We all step through and I pull the door shut, spinning the wheel back in the opposite direction. "Although it's weird it's manually operated."

"Yeah, but the rest is automatic." I place the helmet from the spacesuit onto the floor and pull the suit on over my clothes. Helena and Atticus follow my lead. The suits are clunky, loud, and definitely not fashionable. I help Atticus and Helena get their helmets on once I've clicked mine into place. I tap the receiver on the side of the helmet and turn the radio on.

"We should be good to go," I say to them.

Helena turns to me and tries to say something. I point up at the receiver on her helmet. She taps it then speaks again. "And you're sure this is safe?" Her voice comes over the radio, a little static-y but otherwise crystal clear.

"Perfectly safe!" I make my way over to a small panel on the wall and hit the large button that reads 'AIRLOCK DOOR OPEN'. The door in front of us slides open quietly, revealing a long tunnel behind it. I walk into the next room and over to an identical panel. As soon as Helena and Atticus are inside, I press the button that reads 'AIRLOCK DOOR CLOSE'.

"So beyond that door is… space?" Helena looks down the hallway at the other door.

"Yup. You're gonna love it," I tell her.

"I'm excited." Atticus reaches out and grabs her hand. He fumbles a little bit through the suit but eventually manages to hold her hand. I grab the tethers from the wall and hook them onto the backs of their suits.

"Here, hook this on me." I hand my tether to Atticus and turn around. There's a click as the tether latches onto the back of my suit. I smile at them and hit the button on the control panel to open the far airlock door.

Even through the spacesuit, I can hear the air rushing out of the room and the vacuum tugging on my suit. After a few seconds, the door at the end of the hallway silently slides open, revealing a square of nothingness beyond. I walk down the hallway first, Helena and Atticus following close behind.

"Oh, and one more thing, once we get out there the gravity's gonna feel super weird," I explain.

"Why's that?" Helena asks.

"My guess is it's only designed to work inside the ship. So out on the hull, we only get a bit of it," I explain.

"Sounds dangerous," Helena says.

"Nah, it just means you'll feel a little lighter than usual." I stop walking at the edge of the hallway and look out into the vastness of space. The ship feels so small compared to everything out there. I turn back to Helena and Atticus. "Trust me, this is the fun part." I lean backward and let myself fall into the emptiness of space. The ship spins around me and I feel the gravity shift as I pass the edge of the ship. Dozens of times and the feeling still hasn't gotten old.

"Well, aren't you gonna try it?" I look back down at Helena and Atticus in the open doorway.

"Guess there's no time like the present, huh?" Atticus says and follows suit, slightly less gracefully than me.

"Ok, here goes nothing." Helena goes next, her momentum carrying her upwards to where Atticus and I stand. Atticus catches her as she gets close and they both look around.

"This is absolutely incredible," Helena says.

"Told you it would be. And watch this." I bend down and push off the hull of the ship, propelling myself about thirty feet upwards before floating back down.

"How did you do that?" Helena asks.

"It's the gravity, right?" Atticus says.

"Yup, still here but super light." I tug on the tether. "Plus we've got these here to keep us from going too far," I say. They look at each other quickly before jumping off the ground together, soaring high above me. Their landing is a little rough, ending with both of them in a pile on the hull a little ways ahead of me. They laugh as they pull themselves back up.

"Maybe we should've tried a smaller jump first," Helena says.

"Where's the fun in that?" Atticus grabs her hand and I can't help but notice how much she opens up whenever she's with him.

"So where's this meteor?" I ask.

"Don't you know?" Helena whips around.

"Hey, I just knew about this spot! The meteor is all on you two," I respond.

"It's nothing to worry about, we've still got a little time," Atticus says, turning his gaze out toward the stars. He stares intensely for a couple of seconds before pointing upwards. "There! Do you see it?"

I follow his finger to where he's pointing and see a large shape on the horizon. "Is that it?"

"Should be," he says.

"So what now?" Helena asks.

"We just wait here for it."

"I guess I'll get comfortable." I lay down on the deck and look out at the stars. Even just laying here feels relaxing. I think it's a combination of the silence and not having anyone else around. It's rare to get that anywhere on the ship. Plus, the lower gravity really does feel like a weight has been lifted off me.

I hear music coming over the radio and look up to find where it's coming from. Atticus is playing with the receiver on his helmet. He must've found a way to pick up the signal from somewhere else.

"Oh, I love this song," Helena says, and he stops playing with the receiver, settling on a single frequency.

"I know." Atticus reaches out his hand and Helena takes it. The two of them dance along to the music, gliding effortlessly across the hull of the ship. It's absolutely beautiful watching them. I look back up and find the meteor again, watching as it slowly makes its approach toward the ship.

It takes a long time for the meteor to travel, the songs over the radio change several times as I lay on the deck waiting. I close my eyes for a little bit and just listen. It almost sounds like the show Helena and I went to see at the Proscenium the other night. Suddenly the music cuts off. I open my eyes and sit up to see Atticus and Helena staring up at the meteor. I pull myself up and walk over to join them.

"It's so close," I say.

"Yeah it's probably only about a kilometer or two from the ship," Atticus says.

"It's massive," Helena says.

The meteor doesn't look anything like the ones I've read about in textbooks. Usually, those were all rock and ice but this one looks like it's made from some kind of crystal. The lights from various stars behind it seem to shimmer and refract through the meteor's sharp angles. As the lights shine through, I

catch glimpses of something within the mete-
or. Almost like long dark lines running
throughout the structure.

"What do you think those dark spots
are?" I ask.

"Who knows," Atticus says. "If I had to
guess I'd probably say they were faults that
formed in the crystal structure. Could you
imagine going up and exploring something
like that?" He looks up in awe.

As I stare at it more, I begin to see tiny
specks of light throughout. It's hard to tell if
it's just more stars shining through it or if it's
something within the meteor itself. But the
specks of light look blue and red rather than
the yellow and white of the stars. Before I can
think about it too much, something else
catches my eye.

Beyond the meteor, there's now a large
patch of darkness. Where all the stars used to
be, suddenly there's just... nothing.

"Does anyone else see...?" Helena starts
to say.

"Yeah, I see it too," I say.

"That doesn't look good," Atticus says.
Suddenly the ship lurches upwards, tossing us
a few feet into the air. I look back down at the
hull just in time to see a ripple running along
the metal.

"What was that?" I ask.

"I have no idea. But anything that can move the ship like that can't be good," Atticus says. As soon as the words leave his mouth, there's a horrible screeching sound from behind us. I quickly turn around and see something I can barely wrap my head around.

The lower half of the ship is being twisted off into space. It looks like it's being reflected in a warped mirror. But what could cause the metal to do that? The longer I stare, the worse the shape seems to get. There's a dark patch of space that the hull seems to be moving towards. Just like the one beyond the meteor, there's not a single star inside.

Then all of a sudden the hull snaps back into shape and the void seems to be gone. All the stars are back where they're supposed to be. I look down at the airlock and see a familiar flashing red light letting me know that, once again, the ship is on high alert.

"Whatever that was, we need to go now," I tell Helena and Atticus. The three of us rush back towards the airlock and, as my gut is telling me, towards another ship-wide disaster.

CHAPTER NINE

DEAD IN THE WATER

As I pull myself back into the airlock, the weight of the ship's gravity tugs on me again. Whatever tension had left my body while outside has come rushing back, along with a whole new level from the flashing red lights and blaring alarm.

I quickly close the airlock doors and get us back into the main part of the ship. Once the doors are closed, the three of us take off the spacesuits. I'm out of mine first and immediately run over to the bulkhead to start getting it open. Once Atticus and Helena manage to shed their suits too, they run over to help me with the wheel.

"I've got to get up to the bridge and figure out what's happening," Helena says as soon as we're on the other side of the door.

"What about us?" I ask.

"All I know is that when the ship alarms went off, I wasn't in my room, so my mom is probably freaking out right now." Helena starts running back towards the bridleway and we follow.

"I'm sure it's not that bad," I say.

"Look, either way, I'm still the first officer on this ship so I've got to be up there." We reach the bridleway and she runs into one of the chariots alone. She whispers something to the operator and the chariot shoots up through the bridleway, leaving Atticus and me standing on the empty platform.

I turn to him. "So now what?"

He pauses, a look of deep concern on his face. "Let's get up to the observatory. Maybe we can figure out what's going on," he says. We catch the next chariot and take it up to Deck Six. The walk back to the observatory seems to go much quicker this time but I think that has a lot to do with the blaring alarms and flashing lights.

I clumsily climb down the ladder into the long hallway. The noise of the alarms in the hallway is deafening. Atticus and I rush into the observatory to find everyone there already.

"What's everyone doing down here?" Atticus asks.

"We came down when we heard the alarms," Iris says.

"Do we know what happened?" Nao asks.

"We caught a glimpse of something outside the ship," Atticus says.

"It looked like a big blob of dark. And then it twisted the hull of the ship all out of shape," I add.

"Could that be…?" Iris looks over at Atticus. She has the same look of concern I had seen on his face.

"Yeah, I was thinking that too," he responds.

"Would you two mind filling in the rest of us?" Nao says.

"I think it's a spacial distortion," Atticus says. When he notices how confused some of us look, he clarifies, "It's like a tear in the universe."

"But what does that actually mean?" I ask. The science is a little above my head.

"Short version is that if something collides with one, it could theoretically tear it into another part of the galaxy," Atticus explains.

"So, the hull of the ship getting distorted?"

"Yeah, we probably got close to one and it started to pull the ship apart. We're very lucky it wasn't closer. I can't even imagine what it would've been like if we got pulled into something like that," he says.

"Do you think there are more out there?" Egon finally speaks up.

Iris runs over to one of the computers. "I bet our long-range scanners would be able to map them out for us."

"Do we have any idea what actually happened to the ship?" I ask.

"Didn't you just say we hit one of those anomalies?" Nao says.

"No, I know that, but something must've actually set the alarms off, right? I meant do we have any idea what part of the ship's systems went down?"

"That's a good point—" Atticus starts to say before the entire ship shakes again. This time feels more intense than anything I've ever felt before, maybe even more than when the meteor struck the ship back in my time.

The shaking doesn't stop. Large chunks of the ornately painted ceiling crack and fall to the floor, crumbling into dust. The globe that seemed to float effortlessly in the middle of the room suddenly goes dim and plummets to the ground. Egon and I dive out of its path as it crushes one of the computer stations. Finally, the ship stops shaking.

"Is everyone ok?" Egon asks.

"Yeah, I think I'm ok," Nao says. Everyone looks a little shaken but thankfully no major injuries.

"Well, we've got a bigger problem to deal with," Iris chimes in from her computer station across the room.

"What did you find?" Atticus asks as we all run over, avoiding the twisted heap of metal in the middle of the room that used to be the floating globe. There's a small rectangle on the screen and a series of dark black shapes surrounding it that seem to be continuously changing shape.

"There are more distortions all around the ship," Iris says, pointing at the screen.

"There are dozens of them," Egon says.

"Yeah, but this one is the one that concerns me." Iris points at a shape that dwarfs all the others. "The ship is currently on a direct course with it."

"And what would happen if we hit it straight on?" Nao asks. Iris doesn't say anything, but her face does.

"The ship would be shredded across the entire galaxy in a matter of seconds," Atticus delivers the harsh truth.

Iris turns around and looks over the group of us. "Where's Helena?" she asks, finally realizing she's not here.

"She went up to the bridge," Atticus says.

"So we should be able to listen in, right?" Iris asks.

Nao looks over at one of the stations with a computer. "Yes." As soon as the words have left their mouth, everyone is crowded around the other computer station with Nao. They tap at the controls until a small image appears on the screen. I recognize it instantly as the bridge of the ship.

"We need sound too," Iris says.

"Working on that." Nao continues to tap away at the control panel. I can see Helena and the captain standing around the bridge with what I can only assume are the rest of the senior staff from this time. The sound finally comes through.

"So does that mean we're…?" I hear the captain ask.

"Dead in the water? Yes," another voice says.

"Any chance of repairing the engines?" the captain asks.

"No, we just don't have the tech to fix them anymore," someone else says. Even from here, I can feel how tense the room is.

"Where does that leave us?" the captain asks.

"We'll hit whatever that thing is in about eight hours," the first person says. Silence hangs over both the bridge and the observatory.

"They must be talking about hitting that big spacial distortion," Iris says.

The captain lets out a sigh. "We need to think about worst-case scenarios."

"There aren't really any good options," the other person says.

"We have to consider disembarkation," the captain responds. She sounds completely defeated.

Atticus leans over and mutes the feed from the bridge. "She can't seriously be considering that."

"What's disembarkation?" I ask.

"She wants to launch all the habitats from the ship," Atticus explains.

"Why would that be so bad?"

"Look, all the ship's habitats are designed for short travel, like to transport down to a planet. That's part of why I think the original use of the observatory was to help us find a suitable planet. I can't think of why else they'd only be designed for such short trips," he explains.

"I still don't see why that would be so bad."

"Because we're nowhere near any inhabitable planets. If they launch, they'll just be drifting in space," he says. Nao flips off the video feed from the bridge.

"Yeah, that's not the issue. Sure, it might solve the immediate problem of the space distortions, but the bigger issue is that each habitat can really only support the passengers for a few weeks at most," Iris chimes in.

"And without a planet to land on it's just postponing the inevitable. The truth is we don't have a chance of making it out here in space if we don't have the *Mercury*," Atticus explains.

"And we're sure there's absolutely no planets around?" I ask.

Iris turns back to her screen and points at a small dot in the far corner. "The closest planet to us is this one out here. We scanned it a while back and there's absolutely no atmosphere. Pretty much every planet we've come across seems to be completely dead," she explains.

"So why are they considering disembarkation?" I ask.

"Well, you heard them, we don't have many other choices left, do we?" Atticus says.

"Can there really not be any other options?" Egon chimes in.

"I'm all ears if anyone has any ideas," Atticus says. Everyone stands in silence, the only noise coming from the blaring alarms.

"Could we turn the ship?" I ask.

"They said the engines were completely busted up," Nao says.

"And there's no other way to move the ship?"

"Not unless you want to get out and push," Iris says.

"Iris!" Atticus scolds.

"I'm sorry, Lucy, I didn't mean that. I'm just stressed."

"It's fine," I say.

"She makes a good point, though," Atticus says. Wait, he's not serious about me getting out and pushing, right? "Are there any other ways that we could move the ship somehow?" He seems to be thinking out loud.

"No bad ideas in brainstorming, right?" I joke.

"Look, we'll take any idea we can get right now," Iris says.

"Could we vent the air from a deck into space?" Egon asks.

"It'd be pretty risky," Iris says.

"And might cause us more issues down the road losing that much air off a whole deck," Atticus says. He paces in a small circle as he thinks out loud.

"Plus, who knows how much we'd be able to control something like that. The ship certainly wasn't designed to vent that much air. I wouldn't want to blow a hole in the side of the ship," Iris says.

"Might be better than disembarkation, though. At least with that one, we'd get to keep the *Mercury*. Any other ideas?" Atticus asks.

"What about an explosion?" Nao suggests and Atticus whips around to face them. "The hull is one of the most durable materials in the universe, right? Could an explosion knock us onto another path? Or maybe just get us to stop moving forward?"

"Any ideas on something we could use as an explosive?" Iris asks. I try to think, but nothing comes to mind. Before anyone else can answer, Helena runs into the room looking out of breath.

"I assume you were all watching on the feed?" she asks, and I nod. "I don't know how much you managed to catch but they've decided to move forward with the disembarkation."

"But they can't!" Atticus protests.

"They don't have any other good options!" Helena walks over and gives Atticus a quick kiss on the cheek.

"We're trying to come up with one!" Atticus says.

"And?"

"Nothing just yet," he says sheepishly.

"I might have somewhere we can look," Masumi chimes in for the first time. Everyone turns their attention to her. "There might be something back over in the archives," she says.

Atticus seems to perk up at this idea. "How much access do you have over there?"

"As of this week, full access." Masumi holds up a small key on a gold chain.

"Even the restricted areas?" Iris asks.

"Yes, I'm not just an intern there anymore. I got promoted to assistant archivist, giving me complete access." Masumi smiles.

"Well, congrats on the job. Let's get over there and see what we can find for ideas," Atticus says.

We rush out of the observatory and within minutes we're back up on the deck. I can see the giant marble building of the archive in the distance. Everyone runs toward it and I try my best to keep up. Moving on the new leg has gotten easier but my running is still a little uneven. Egon could easily be at the front of the group, but he makes a point to hang back and run with me.

"You doing ok?" he asks.

"Yeah, I'm just not as quick as I used to be," I say.

"Nor do you need to be. I will stay with you," he says as we run together. The others pull a little further ahead but I feel better having Egon with me. They reach the archives about two minutes ahead of us and are standing at the top of a short marble staircase.

Egon and I climb up the steps and meet them at the massive front doors which sit between the large marble columns. The wooden doors have delicate-looking figures carved throughout their entire height. I can't imagine how long it must've taken to make these.

"Do we have to avoid anyone while we're here?" Nao asks.

"No, I should be the only one here at this time. There's not often anyone who comes here in the middle of the night," Masumi explains.

"Yeah, guessing during an emergency the archives probably aren't anyone's top destination," Iris says.

Masumi pushes on the doors and they swing inwards, revealing the archives. I don't think I've actually set foot in here since I was a little kid on a field trip, but it hasn't changed a bit. The bookshelves stretch up to the ceilings, stuffed to the brim with thousands of old books. The floors and the ceilings are paneled in dark brown wood, and at the end of each aisle is a small marble statue on a pedestal, each adorned with little brass plaques.

We make our way down the main room to a smaller small set of wooden doors at the far end. When we reach the doors, Masumi pulls out the chain with the key and slips it into the golden lock. There's a soft click and the doors swing inward.

I step forward into the restricted area of the archives. I don't know why I was expecting something a little more spectacular, but this feels a little anticlimactic. It's just a small room with a couple wooden cabinets and drawers. There are a few tables in the middle, but compared to the main room it's not very impressive.

"Kind of a letdown," Nao says. I blurt out a laugh.

"Glad I'm not the only one who thinks that," I say. Nao gives me a smile.

"So where should we start?" Egon asks.

"We should look for any information about the ship itself," Iris says.

"Yeah, at this point we're looking for a Hail Mary option," Atticus says.

We disperse and frantically start pulling open drawers. I pull one open that has various old paintings laying on top of each other, not even in frames. The first canvas has a bright yellow vase with sunflowers in it. Egon would probably like it. I lift up the fabric and look at the one underneath. It almost looks like the cafes back in the residential area of the ship, complete with the cobblestone streets and tables sitting outside. I doubt these are what we're looking for so I slide the drawer closed and check another one.

The next drawer doesn't give me much better luck. Looks like a bunch of old maps, but none that I can recognize any details of. As I'm about to move onto the third drawer, Atticus calls out to us.

"I think I found something." He holds a large piece of paper above his head before slamming it down on the table. I walk over and look at the paper.

"No way," I say.

"What is it?" Atticus asks.

"Uh… nothing." I quickly bite my tongue. This is the exact same set of blueprints I found in my mother's quarters back in my time. Or, more accurately, these are the blueprints I stole from her quarters and used to guide my expedition into the quarantined section of the ship.

"What's so important about these?" Iris asks.

"Look what it says right here — Warp Core." Atticus points at the center of the blueprints.

"What's a warp core?" Nao asks. They look just as confused as the rest of us.

"It's an old piece of tech. Developed back around the same time as the early space missions. I've read about them in history books, but I didn't know our ship was equipped with one," Atticus explains.

"Why's it important, though?" I ask.

"It's because of how those warp cores actually work. They distort space and allow the ship to pass through huge distances in an instant."

"So can we use it to move the ship?" Egon asks.

"That might be too risky. There's still a chance we could hit one of the distortions. But I think we might be able to use it to get rid of the big one," Atticus says. "I think if we can create our own massive wave in space-time we might be able to nullify the one we're drifting towards."

"So do we just turn on the warp core at full blast?" Egon asks.

"No, the core is too far in the middle of the ship. I'm afraid by the time the actual core is inside the distortion, the ship would already have been torn apart. the *Mercury* is just too big," Atticus explains.

"What do you need?" Iris asks.

"We need to remove the warp core and get it into the middle of the distortion on its own." Atticus looks over the blueprints of the ship again. Then a thought occurs to me.

"I think I may know how we can get it out there," I say. "What if we sent it out in one of those old shuttles?"

"What shuttles?" Iris asks.

"She means one of the old survey ships. We found them earlier," Atticus says.

"Wait, you found them?" Iris asks.

"Yes. You know, that could really work," Atticus says. He pulls out a pencil and starts frantically scribbling notes onto the map. The exact same notes I used to find the quarantined section back in my time. So they really did come from him.

"You really think so?" I ask.

"I do. Although it's still going to be a lot of work. Those survey crafts didn't look like they were in the best shape when we saw them earlier. We'll need to fix them up," Atticus says.

"I can start fixing one of the shuttles up," Egon says.

"Good, thank you, Egon. Nao, would you be able to help Egon get the shuttle ready and make sure we can launch from the airlock?" Atticus asks.

"Yeah, we can go down with him and help out with that," Nao says.

"Ok good, the shuttle bay is down on Deck Eleven at the end of the unfinished section. I'm hoping the guard will have cleared out too. Oh, and Masumi, can you get into the ship's systems? I want to know everything that's going on," Atticus says.

"Yes, I will head back to the observatory and stay in contact with you," Masumi says.

"Iris, I need you to rig up a system to activate the warp core and coat the shuttle in a warp bubble. It's gonna be a little tough," Atticus says.

Iris smiles at him. "Maybe tough for you."

"Good. Helena, Lucy, and I will go down to get the warp core and meet you back at the shuttle bay." Atticus carefully folds up the blueprints and hands them to Helena.

"Let's hurry," Helena says. The three of us part ways with the others and make our way up to the Lido Deck.

CHAPTER TEN

298B

The lights continue to flash as the ship's alarm echoes through the deck. It had been muffled slightly by the thick marble walls of the archive but the second we're outside again it's back to full volume, possibly even louder than before. We follow the winding path back up towards the bridleway and as we're waiting for the next chariot to appear, a voice cuts through the alarm.

"ATTENTION RESIDENTS OF THE *MERCURY*. PLEASE PROCEED TO HABITATS. DISEMBARKMENT PROTOCOL NOW INITIATED," the captain's booming voice echoes throughout the deck.

"So they're really moving ahead with it," Atticus says.

"I told you they were," Helena responds.

"Yeah, I guess I was just hoping they'd keep looking for another way," he says.

"Why don't we tell them about what we're trying?" I ask.

"We can't risk that they'll shut us down. We can tell them once we've completed it," Atticus says.

Usually, the chariots that run this late are completely empty but the one that pulls up this time is packed full of people. We squeeze into the pod and I can feel the nervous energy of the families inside, all carrying bags and an assortment of household objects. Clearly they had to grab stuff in a hurry and tried to gather as many important things as they possibly could.

"This is going to be a mess," Atticus whispers to me and Helena. I nod in agreement, remembering the chaos of the ship in my time when the meteor hit it. Many of the people around us look like they didn't even have time to change out of their pajamas. The chariot operator looks a little nervous too.

The chariot barely sides into the station before people start to push towards the doors. As soon as they open, the crowd stampedes out, nearly trampling the three of us. Someone grabs my arm and pulls me out of the way. I look up and see that Atticus managed to pull me and Helena to safety.

"Let's keep moving," he says, dropping my hand but still holding onto Helena's. I run after him as he sprints toward the Lido Deck. The rest of the deck has completely erupted into chaos and we seem to be running in the opposite direction of almost every other person. After about ten minutes, I see the large sign for the Lido Deck. The small cafeteria is completely deserted as we run inside.

"Looks like everyone's evacuated from here already," I say.

We leave the cafeteria and emerge onto the Lido Deck. It looks just like the first time I was here. Not a soul in sight, no water left in the pools, and an unnerving vibe around the whole room. My footsteps echo loudly as we run. I can see whole plates of food stacked on the bar, completely untouched. People's towels and pool accessories lay scattered on the ground, left there by the fleeing crowds.

There's suddenly a loud creaking noise throughout the room, audible even over the blaring alarms. Atticus stops and looks up towards the ceiling. I look up too. The glass roof seems different somehow.

"Don't move at all," Atticus says. That's when I notice what about the glass looks different. There are no stars beyond it, just darkness.

"It's a distortion, isn't it?" I ask, my heart racing.

"Yes. We have to be very careful right now," he says. Slowly, the glass starts to ripple like water. It continues for a few seconds before finally stopping. We wait a few seconds more in complete silence.

"Ok, I think we should be good again. Can I see the blueprints?" Atticus breaks the silence, turning to Helena.

"Sure, here you go." She pulls them out of her pocket and passes them over to Atticus. He unfolds the papers and looks around the room.

"It looks like there's some kind of maintenance tunnels that we can access from this wall." He walks over to the far end of the Lido Deck. "I just have to find the panel." He starts poking at each one separately.

I immediately walk over to the metal panel that has the small handle and tug the panel open, revealing the dark room beyond it. "It's over here."

Atticus looks puzzled. "How did you know it was there?"

"I got a look at the map earlier," I say. His eyes narrow and I can tell he doesn't believe me.

"Let's get going then," Helena interrupts before he can question me further, but something tells me he's not ready to let the conversation go just yet.

We squeeze through the open panel one at a time, which is definitely a lot easier to do without the bulky spacesuit like the last time I was here. The lights flicker before turning on, revealing the same long walkway and massive pipes stretching throughout the room.

Fortunately, the alarms and flashing lights don't seem to be going off in here.

"Wow, this is incredible." Atticus walks forwards and marvels at the room.

"These must run the entire length of the ship," Helena says, looking down at all the pipes. More lights turn on as we walk forward, revealing the rest of the walkway. The pipe that once blocked the path is no longer there, leaving the sphere ahead of us clearly visible. But there's one noticeable difference which is that it seems to be glowing with a faint blue light. The pipes coming out of the sphere also pulse with the same blue light. I watch the pulses as they travel down the pipes, casting a blue glow on their surroundings.

The thick metal door slams loudly as I open it and blue light pours out of the room.

"What's that weird light?" Helena asks.

"It must be the warp core," Atticus says. I follow him into the room. The once pure-white room is now filled with bright blue light reflecting off the walls. It's almost blinding. I can barely make out the pedestal in the center, but I feel my way toward it.

"Please enter user credentials," the AI panel chimes to life as my fingers brush up against it.

"These must be the controls for the warp core," Atticus says, finding his way over to me.

"How do we get it out?" Helena asks. My eyes finally start to adjust to the bright light.

"It probably needs an ID," Atticus says.

"Let's use mine," she says. "After all there shouldn't be much on this ship that the first officer doesn't have access to." She reaches into her jacket and pulls out her ID badge, tapping it onto the panel. There's no mistaking it either, it's the exact same badge I currently have tucked into my pocket. Although mine looks a little more worn than hers does right now.

"Insufficient privilege," the little AI voice says.

"Why wouldn't I have access to this?" Helena asks.

"It's probably only the captain that has full access here," Atticus says.

"Well, as soon as we're out of here I'm gonna make sure I have access to everything on the ship too."

"Then how do we get in?" I ask.

"We might be able to cut power to this whole room," Atticus says. "Helena, would you mind checking to see if there's any power box outside? It would probably be back near the beginning of the walkway."

"Yeah, sure," Helena says. She goes back out through the door we came in. Atticus and I stand on either side of the panel without saying anything. Wait, she said she was going to give herself access, right? And if the ID in my pocket really is the same one, does that mean it already has access?

"I think I might have something that would work." I pull out the ID from my pocket and tap it against the panel, careful to hide it from Atticus' view.

There's a ping from the panel. "Credentials accepted. Welcome, First Officer Inez," it announces. A series of commands appear on the panel. START ENGINE. STOP ENGINE. ENGINE DIAGNOSTIC. OPEN WARP CONTAINER. CLOSE WARP CONTAINER. ENGINE INFORMATION. "Please choose a command," the panel says.

Atticus looks up at me. "So, Lucy, can I ask you something?"

"Sure," I say, but I already have a pretty good idea of what he's about to ask.

"Do you know us in the future?" Even still, his question catches me off guard.

"W-what?" I stutter, trying to cover a little bit.

"Look, I've been trying to give you space about it, but I also see the way you act around us," he says. I feel my face turning red. I was worried he had started to piece it together and looks like I was right.

"What do you mean?" I try to play it off.

"Call it a feeling, but you seem to know more than you're letting on. Even earlier with that panel to get in here. You walked straight towards it with no hesitation, like you've been here before."

I doubt I can outsmart him but maybe I can at least try. "I told you, I saw it on the map."

"And now this." He moves quickly, grabs the old ID badge out of my hands, and looks it over. He stops as soon as he sees the picture of Helena. "It's her." He looks over to the door where Helena is, still looking for an electrical box, too far away to hear our conversation.

"Atticus, please," I plead.

"No, I just saw this in her hand. How did you get it? And why did it work for you and not her?"

"It's really nothing," I say.

"Just tell me how you know us!" He says it loudly, but it's not anger in his voice. No, it's more like pleading. For the guy who likes to know everything, I can see how much it's killing him not to know something. Especially something about him.

"I don't know you in the future," I say, the words barely making it out. "But I always wanted to."

"What are you talking about?"

I peer back outside quickly before looking him in the eyes. "Helena is my mom." I hesitate for a second before letting the other shoe drop. "And you're my father."

"What?" He looks completely shocked. I can hardly blame him either. It's not like I handled it much better after our first interaction. Even still I'm barely holding it together.

"I didn't want you to find out this way." I can feel myself getting choked up.

"What do you mean I'm your father? How is that even possible?" he asks.

"I thought you believed that I was from the future," I say.

"Being from the future is one thing! But telling me you're my daughter, that's just… a lot…" He looks away and his eyes glance down to the ID in his hand. He turns back and holds the ID up to my face, his eyes darting between Helena's picture and me. "And you…" I see the realization cross his face.

"I'm so sorry, I shouldn't have told you like this. I just always really wanted to meet you." The tears are streaming down my face. I should've just left it.

"So does that mean… you haven't met me before?" Crap. I wasn't thinking.

"Wait, no, I didn't mean… I just meant…" I'm too much of a mess to find the right words.

"Does something happen to me in the future?"

"I… I don't…"

"Lucy, I need to know!" he says, his voice rising again.

"You died, ok?"

Silence.

Those were the exact wrong words. I could have said anything else. Why didn't I say something else? He looks completely devastated.

"Atticus, I'm so sorry." My voice is barely louder than a whisper.

"How?" he asks.

"What?"

"How does it happen?"

"I don't know. She never gave me the details."

"You mean Helena?"

I nod. "She doesn't like to talk about it. I've tried but I can tell it's too painful for her."

Everything else melts away in the silence between us. All the talk of the warp core, fixing the ship, and passing meteors fades away. Nothing else seems to exist right now.

He finally breaks the silence. "So that first time we met, and you ran off…"

"Yeah, it was just a little overwhelming," I admit.

"I know how you feel." He gives me a very forced smile. The kind of smile you give someone when you're holding back tears. There's a pause where neither of us says anything again.

"I shouldn't have told you," I say.

"No, I suppose it's good you did." He seems distracted. Understandably so.

"In what possible way?"

"Well, Helena's still alive in your time, right?"

"Yeah, but you're not," I remind him.

"Is she ok, though?"

I think about that a little bit. Is she? I mean, she's nothing like the Helena I've been hanging out with in this time. But she still runs the ship, right? "I think so…" I don't sound very convincing.

"I really hope she is. All I want is for her to be happy." He really means that, doesn't he?

"I don't understand how you're ok with this!"

"I wouldn't say I'm fully ok with it. I'm definitely still trying to wrap my brain around it."

It's a selfish thought but it still manages to come out of my lips. "But we never get to meet!"

"But we did get to meet now, right? Sure, it's not in the right order but it's got to count for something."

"I guess…"

He smiles a little. "You know, she asked me the other week if I would ever want to have kids."

"Why would she ask that?"

"Well at the time I thought it was purely a hypothetical question, but now I'm thinking there may have been a little more behind it."

"What do you mean?" I ask. He says nothing but raises his eyebrow knowingly. That's when it clicks. She knows she's pregnant.

"Now you're getting it." He nods. "Either way, I told her I was on board. I always wanted a kid." His tone is bittersweet.

And I realize he's right. It may not have been how I imagined it would happen, and certainly not in any order that makes sense, but after all these years I did get to know who my dad was. "I'm glad I finally got to meet you."

"Yeah, me too. I hope I didn't disappoint," he jokes.

"You could never." I give him a big hug and he hugs me back. I know I have to but there's a part of me that thinks if I don't let him go then nothing can happen to him, right? As unrealistic as that is, I know it's completely irrational. I finally pull away.

"And, hey, there's one good piece of news about this," he says with a smile.

"What's that?" My voice is a little choked up from all the crying.

"Our plan is going to work. Because you're here and Helena was alive in the future it already has worked."

And almost as if on cue, Helena comes back into the room. She looks at our faces with a puzzled expression. "Did I miss something?"

Atticus walks up and wraps his arms around her, kissing her deeply. She giggles.

I awkwardly look away, wiping some of the tears from my eyes which luckily Helena doesn't seem to notice. "We got the panel working."

Helena pulls away from Atticus. "Oh, that's perfect!" She runs over and looks at the readout of the controls.

"Let's try this one." Atticus taps the screen where it says OPEN WARP CONTAINER.

"Warp container opening," the panel pings. The top of the pedestal slides open silently revealing a glowing blue hexagon. I reach towards it and as my hand gets close, I feel a wave of cold radiating off it, along with the blue light.

"It's cold," I say. I grab the edges of the hexagon and pull it upwards out of the pedestal only to find that it's attached by a series of wires and small tubes.

"We need to cut it out," Atticus says.

Helena watches us nervously. "Is that safe?"

"I checked the blueprints pretty carefully and this should only affect the ship's ability to warp anywhere. None of the other ship's systems should be affected. And, honestly, losing warp seems like a fine price to pay for keeping the ship in one piece," Atticus says. He pulls a small blade from his pocket and starts cutting the wires and tubes around the warp core. As he slices through them, they spark and wave around frantically. Some of the wires touch each other and melt together, leaving a twisted nest within the pedestal. He finally cuts through the last tube and the blue light slowly fades from the room.

"Let's move," he says. We leave the room and run back down the walkway. I catch a glimpse of his face when he thinks I'm not looking and see an expression I haven't seen on him before. But based on our last conversation I piece together what he might be thinking about. I'd probably guess the emotion was something like dread mixed with panic and anxiety.

The pipes that were pulsing blue before are now fading just like the room. The only glow now comes from the warp core I've got tucked under my arm. As the large pipes stop glowing, I hear them start to creak and move. I also hear something directly above us and look up just in time to see a section of pipe falling toward us.

"RUN," I yell, pushing Atticus and Helena forward. The three of us dive out of the way as the pipe crashes into the walkway, shaking it violently. I look back and see it laying across the walkway, just like it was in my time.

"We have to get out of here," Atticus says. We pull ourselves up and continue running down the hallway. We squeeze back out onto the Lido Deck and I pull the panel tightly shut behind us.

We sprint through the empty deck, avoiding all the junk people left strewn over the ground. The ship shakes violently and all of us are knocked to the ground. I'm careful to try and protect the warp core with my body. I don't know what would happen if it broke but something tells me it wouldn't be a fun outcome.

I slam into the ground and feel a shooting pain through my arm. Damn it. The bruise on that arm had just faded too. I go to pull myself up and suddenly feel light. Did I hit my head?

Then I realize what's happened. The gravity on this deck is no longer on. All the junk people had left around is floating up- wards along with the multitudes of vending machines, beach umbrellas, and half-finished cocktails at the bar. I tuck the warp core in- side my jacket and zip it up before reaching out and grabbing hold of the nearest vending machine.

"Well, hello there! Is there anything I can assist you with today?" the machine asks. If possible, it seems even more chipper than the last time I saw it. I don't respond. I'm not gonna give it anything to work with this time. I look around for Atticus and Helena. They're floating a couple of feet above me. It looks like neither of them managed to grab onto anything before the gravity switched off.

"Lucy!" Atticus yells. He's almost direct- ly above me. "You need to get us down."

"How? I don't see a way to reach you!"

He points at the bar. "There should be a fire extinguisher over at the bar. You need to use that to move yourself around the room," he shouts.

I look over at the bar and see a large red fire extinguisher mounted to the wall. "That's ridiculous!" I call back.

"I didn't ask for your opinion," he says. I push off of the vending machine towards the fire extinguisher and grab it off the wall as I float by. I press down on the button near the hose and a thick white foam sprays out. The force of it pushes me backward, away from the bar.

"Good, now use that to come get us down. And hurry," Atticus demands. Like he'd be any better at this. I slowly twist around and spray foam toward the ground. It pushes me upwards and seconds later my head collides with Atticus's gut. He lets out a breath as I knock into him.

"Give me that," he says as he takes the fire extinguisher. "And grab my ankle." I do as he says, and he quickly gets us moving toward Helena. "You ok?" he asks once we're near her.

"Yeah, just a little dizzy," she says. She grabs hold of him and before I can even really process what's going on we're moving in the direction of the doorway.

"How'd you do that?" I ask, watching him fly us around the room effortlessly.

"Story for another time." There's a slight smile on his face when he says this.

"It's a good one too." Helena smiles at him and they laugh together. We reach the doorway to the cafeteria only to find one of the emergency bulkhead doors blocking the way. Atticus pulls out a small radio from his pocket.

"Masumi, are you there?" he asks into the radio.

There's a bit of static before a voice responds. "Atticus, is that you?" she asks.

"Yes, did you manage to get into the ship's control systems?"

"Of course, did you get the warp unit?"

"We did, but we've got a problem," Atticus says. "We got cut off by bulkheads trying to get out of the Lido Deck. We need these open if we're going to make it out of here." He sounds a little more frantic now.

"Ok, let me see what I can do," she says. There's silence from the radio.

"You think she can get it?" Helena asks.

"I trust her," Atticus says.

Masumi's voice comes through the radio again, "We've got a bit of an issue. All the ship's power is being diverted to the disembarkation protocols. It looks like that's why they shut off the gravity in that whole section."

"What's that mean for us?" Atticus asks.

"I can only re-route enough power to open one bulkhead at a time," she explains.

"Ok, well let's try and go as quick as we can."

"What's the number on the first door?" she asks.

"299B." Atticus reads off the large red letters painted on the bulkhead door. There's a pause before the bulkhead slides upwards. We float through a couple of feet before finding another bulkhead blocking our way.

"Ok, we're through," Atticus says.

"Good, closing 299B," Masumi says. The door behind us slides shut. "What's the next one?"

"Bulkhead 299A." A pause, then the next door opens, and we continue into the room. As we do, I'm pulled towards the floor. Guess we must be getting back to a part of the ship where the gravity's still on. Atticus pulls out his radio. "Close 299A." The bulkhead shuts behind us. There is a loud creaking from the metal ceiling.

"You two go first," Atticus says. I look around the room to see various utensils floating with the lower gravity. I think back to the first time I was in this room, surrounded by these same utensils. Atticus snaps me back to attention before the thought can fully finish.

"Keep moving! We need to get out of here ASAP," he says as he pushes me forward. It's slow progress moving over the ground with the limited gravity, but we keep going. Helena reaches the next bulkhead first.

"Bulkhead 298B open, please," Atticus says into the radio. The bulkhead opens and I go through. I get into the next hallway right behind Helena, then turn around to see Atticus standing in the center of the cafeteria.

"What's he doing over there?" Helena asks, standing just outside the bulkhead.

"I don't know," I say. He's staring up at the mural on the ceiling. "What are you doing, Atticus?" I shout over to him. Then my eyes drift up to the ceiling and I see what has him transfixed. The metal is warping outwards, distorting the murals until the images are completely unrecognizable. I remember what it looked like in my time and the pieces click together. Atticus quickly raises the radio to his mouth.

"ATTICUS, NO," I scream as I realize what he's about to do. I grab Helena by her collar and pull her through the doorway.

"Close bulkhead 298B," he says. The bulkhead between us and him slams shut. There's a screeching metallic noise and I run to the window on the door. Atticus looks over to me and Helena, raises the radio to his mouth, and says something into it. There's a big dopey grin on his face and tears in his eyes. The screeching noise is suddenly magnified as the ceiling of the cafeteria rips open and Atticus is tossed out into the void of space.

CHAPTER ELEVEN

34 SECONDS

My heart feels like it's been ripped out of my chest. Time passes in slow motion as Helena collapses in tears beside me. I can't move. My entire body is paralyzed in place. I can't even manage to speak. As the screeching of metal disappears, I hear the quiet sobbing of Helena on the floor, barely audible above the blaring alarm.

I can feel the tears rolling down my face too. It's not fair. I had to wait my whole life to meet him and once I finally do, he's gone again, just like that. I should've done something more. I should have found another way to get the warp core out instead of going through that stupid cafeteria. As the grief washes over me, I collapse to the ground beside Helena.

Neither of us speaks. We just sit there and cry. I can feel the cold radiating off of the warp core inside my jacket. We may have gotten it safely out, but it feels like a hollow victory. I look over and see the makeup running down Helena's face. The same makeup she spent all that time putting on just so she'd look cute for Atticus.

"Helena…" My throat feels like there's something lodged in it.

"Don't," she cuts me off.

"I just—"

"I SAID DON'T," she snaps at me tearfully, looking for someone to direct her emotions at. I look away, unsure what to say next. We sit in silence for another few minutes. I pull out the warp core and look it over, checking to make sure it didn't get damaged through all the commotion.

Helena catches a glimpse of it and scoffs. "What a damn waste."

"What do you mean?"

"We should've just left that thing where it was." She glares at the warp core with a gaze that tells me she'd much rather we smash it to pieces.

"We can still save the ship, though," I try to gently remind her.

"How can you even think about anything else right now?" Her gaze turns to me in a look of disgust.

"Because he saved us," I say.

"What?"

"Atticus did what he did to get us out of there. So that we could go save the rest of the ship."

"Don't you dare say his name again." Her tear-filled eyes stare directly into mine. All the vibrance I had seen in them over the past few weeks is gone. And they look familiar. In fact, I'd know them anywhere, they're my mother's eyes. The same eyes that would scold me when I got in trouble. But I see them differently now. All this time I had thought I was just seeing anger behind them, but it wasn't anger at all, it was grief.

"What about the rest of the ship?" I try to think of something to pull her back. To stop the grief from consuming her. But it's hard to think of something while trying to swallow my own grief. And it's not like I can share what his loss means to me either, not now. It would be too much for her, too much for me even.

She hangs her head and stares at the floor. "I don't care anymore."

"But if we don't do something we'll die too."

"Why would I want to live without him?" The tears have dried up from her face and now she just seems... defeated. Like any life she had in her died the second Atticus did.

"You've still got your friends," I remind her, but she doesn't respond. Pulling myself up from the floor takes all the strength I can muster. It feels like the ship's gravity has increased tenfold. Yeah, that must be it. The tears roll down my face again.

Without the radio, the two of us are trapped between the bulkhead doors. I look around until I finally see a small panel on the wall next to the far door. When I pull it open a bundle of wires falls out but that doesn't exactly give me any leads on how to open the door.

"Do you know how to open this bulkhead?" I look down at Helena, but she says nothing. Won't even look up at me. My heart sinks. I guess I've really lost her, haven't I?

I look back at the wires sticking out of the panel. I mean, it's not like things can get much worse, right? I start ripping out the wires one by one, waiting to see if anything happens with them. Each torn wire sends sparks flying. Finally, one seems to do the trick. The bulkhead rises a few feet before holding in place. It's not a lot but it looks just wide enough to crawl under.

"Come on." I drag Helena over to the bulkhead. Her arm hangs limply at her side like she's lost all will to move on her own. I push her underneath the door, carefully crawling through after her.

Once we're on the other side I stand up and pull her to her feet. We stand there, surrounded by the chaos of hundreds of people running around the deck. Helena stares straight ahead.

"I'm done," she says quietly, still staring into nothing, the same vacant look on her face.

"What do you mean you're done?" I ask.

"With all of it. With that damn warp core. With all those others down in the observatory. We never should have meddled. We're not really scientists, it was just some silly name we gave ourselves. But we did meddle, and look where it got us? Well, I'm done," she says bitterly. She starts to walk away and I grab her hand, making one last-ditch attempt to bring her back. But as she pulls her hand away from mine, I feel her slip through my fingers.

"Helena…"

"Don't come after me." She turns and walks away, disappearing into the crowd within seconds.

I look down at my empty hand. Should I have gone after her? I don't know what I'm supposed to do anymore. I suddenly feel very alone in this time, realizing I don't have anyone I can go to for help. The chaos of the ship seems to fade away around me.

As if I'm on autopilot, my feet carry me back to the bridleway and I ride one of the chariots down. People push and bump into me, but they barely even register. My brain feels fuzzy, and I find myself unable to keep a single thought in my head. The whole trip down to the shuttle bay goes by in a haze.

"Lucy! Where are Helena and Atticus?" Iris's voice snaps me back to attention.

"They…" I feel the tears welling up again.

"Lucy! Where are they?" I can hear it in her voice, she's definitely impatient.

"They're… gone…"

And as if she suddenly notices that I'm about to cry, her gaze softens. "What do you mean they're gone?"

"Helena ran off somewhere and Atticus…" I start crying again. "He'd dead."

There's silence between us as I watch Iris absorb the information. As the gears click inside her head, I see despair appear on her face.

"That can't be, are you sure?" she pleads, desperate for another answer, like her brain won't accept the one I just gave her.

"There was a distortion and it pulled him out into space," I say through my tears. Even just talking about it brings the memories of that moment flooding back. Iris starts crying and I give her a big hug. We stand there for a few minutes, the warp core in my jacket digging awkwardly into my ribs.

Apparently, she must've felt it too because when she pulls away, she asks, "What's in your jacket?"

I pull out the glowing warp core and hand it to her. "This."

"You found it." She turns it over in her hands, the blue light illuminating her face and reflecting off the big goggles on her head.

"Now what?" I ask, hoping she'll have some idea of what to do.

She looks over to the shuttle with sparks flying off of it. "We have to tell them."

I follow Iris over to the shuttle where Egon and Nao are busy at work. They've made a lot of progress in the hours since we've been gone. The two of them stop their work and run over excitedly once they notice us.

"Is that the warp core?" Nao asks.

"We need to talk," Iris says solemnly.

"Where are Atticus and Helena?" Egon notices their absence right away and I see the look of concern on his face. There's a pause, neither Iris nor myself wanting to be the one to break the news. Like somehow not saying it will make it a little less real.

But finally, I realize someone has to tell them. "Atticus is dead."

Instantly the mood shifts from excitement to despair. I can see Nao struggling to grasp this. But Egon's expression is what makes me burst into tears again. He's the only one who knows what losing Atticus really meant to me and his knowing gaze is too much for me to handle. I sob and, like a dam breaking, within seconds the rest of the group is too. The four of us cry for what feels like an hour before we're just standing there in silence again.

Nao, still with tears in their eyes, speaks first. They sound completely defeated at this point. "So, what do we do now?"

"We may be in over our head," Iris says, trying to pull herself together.

"Why's that?" Nao asks.

"Even with the warp core we still have one big issue with our plan," Iris says.

"What?" I ask.

"It's the shuttle. There's not enough time to build an automated system. We'll be able to get the warp unit in there and get it functional but that's all we had time to build." Iris looks up at the shuttle looming next to us.

"So, what does that mean?" I try to wrap my head around what she's saying but I'm only half there.

"It means someone has to actually be in there to activate the warp core," Nao explains.

We all stand there awkwardly until I finally ask the question that I'm sure we were all just thinking. "Who goes?"

"Well, unfortunately we have no way of knowing what's going to happen once the shuttle gets into the distortion. It might end up being a one-way trip," Iris says. I look up at the shuttle, the exterior of which has been hastily welded together with a bunch of scrap panels. Around the shuttle sits little piles of various machinery and equipment that looks like it was stripped out of the inside of the craft.

"Do we call it here?" Nao asks. We all weigh that question heavily. It's certainly a valid question. After all, we have no idea if this plan is going to work and we've already gotten someone killed for it. Maybe we really are in over our heads. Maybe Helena was right, and we shouldn't have meddled.

But I remember Atticus standing there in the cafeteria, that big dumb grin on his face. He closed that airlock for us. For me, for Helena, for the rest of the ship. If we give up now then what did he even die for?

"No," I say.

"Why not? We don't even know if it's really going to work," Nao says.

I think back to the conversation I had in the warp core room with Atticus. "It has to work," I say. "Because the ship is still there in my time." Just like Atticus said. We already know it's going to work since I've already been there.

And after a while of not speaking, Egon finally chimes in with the answer to the question that none of us wanted to acknowledge. "I'll fly it."

Iris looks completely shocked. "Are you sure?"

"Yes, I know the controls the best out of anyone here," Egon says. I walk over and give him a big hug. As I do, Masumi comes running into the shuttle bay.

"We've got a problem," she says. She's completely out of breath, like she just ran here from the observatory. "Helena told the captain."

Damn. I knew she was upset but I didn't think she'd do something like that.

"The security team is already on the way down here to shut this whole project down," Masumi says.

"We have to move NOW," Iris shouts at everyone. Nao and Egon run back over to the shuttle and begin welding more panels onto the sides. Iris sprints over to the shuttle door and runs inside. I quickly follow her and find her kneeling on a hexagonal panel on the floor. She starts plugging a bunch of tubes and cables into the warp core until it looks exactly like it did before we took it out of the other room.

"What can I do?" I ask. I watch her work on the warp core but, honestly, I don't know how I could possibly help.

"Start barricading the door," she says.

I run back out of the shuttle and see that Masumi has already started stacking objects in front of the door to the shuttle bay. I grab anything I can get my hands on and start adding it to the piles.

"Do you know how long we've got?" I ask.

"Half an hour at most," she responds.

"Damn, that's not very long." We grab a nearby table and stand it up on its side in front of the door. As we're stacking, there's suddenly a loud pounding from the other side of the door.

Masumi looks over at me nervously. "I may have been a little off in my estimate."

"They're here!" I yell over to the others.

"Get back from the door." Iris comes back out of the shuttle covered in what looks like machine oil. Masumi and I run back to join the others just before there's a massive pulse that shakes the room and scatters the pile Masumi and I had made throughout the room in a thick cloud of white smoke. I hear heavy boots on the floor and as the smoke begins to clear I see the green uniforms of the security team.

Among the crowd of security officers, there's a figure who stands a full head taller than everyone else. The captain walks out of the smoke, her pure white uniform looking crisp and pressed despite just having blown a

hole through the wall. And she looks absolutely furious.

"WHAT THE HELL IS GOING ON
HERE?" she screams at us. I and the others
shrink back from her. She takes a few steps
towards us, her shoes clicking on the metal
floor.

"We can't let her get the shuttle," Iris
whispers to me.

"Agreed," I say.

"You see that big red button over by the
wall?" she asks. I look over and see the button on the far side of the room. "That will
shut the shuttle off from this side of the room.
You need to press it and get back over before
the blast door closes."

"I SAID, WHAT IS GOING ON?" the
captain yells even louder. Even her security
staff seems to shrink away from her now.

"We're trying to save the ship!" Iris responds. The captain stares daggers through
her.

"Oh yes, Helena told me about your little
plan. And I'm here to put an end to it." She
steps aside to reveal Helena standing with her.
But not the same Helena I had just been with.
No, the fun outfit she had worn before is
gone, replaced by a perfectly pressed first
officer's uniform. For the first time since getting here, she really looks like my mother.

"Helena! How could you?" Iris screams.

"She did the right thing!" the captain responds.

Iris leans in closer to me and whispers, "When I create a distraction, you need to run and hit the button."

"What are the two of you whispering about?" the captain snaps.

"This!" Iris sprints towards Helena, tackling her to the ground. The second she does, I take off sprinting in the opposite direction, toward the button.

"Stop her!" The captain yells, but I've already got a head start. I hear the security officers behind me and when I turn to look back, I see Egon, Nao, and Masumi stepping in to hold them off. A few more steps and I reach the button. I slam my fist into it and hear a voice over the speakers.

"SHUTTLE BAY LAUNCH PROCEDURES ACTIVATED," the voice says. Without more warning than that, a massive bulkhead door, the entire length of the room, drops from the ceiling, splitting the room in half.

"EXTERIOR DOOR OPENING IN THIRTY SECONDS, TWENTY-NINE, TWENTY-EIGHT," the automated voice starts counting down. I look over at the exterior wall and my heart sinks. I'm on the wrong side of the airlock. I panic and look around to see the only thing left in this half of the room with me — the shuttle.

That'll have to do. I sprint over to the shuttle like my life depends on it, which I guess in this case it does. I pull the door firmly shut behind me just in time to hear the exterior airlock of the shuttle bay open.

The vacuum of space pulls all the air out of the bay and, along with it, the shuttle. The force of it being knocked out into space sends me flying painfully into one of the walls. I'm disoriented but I manage to pull myself up and look out the tiny window. The *Mercury* is getting further and further away from me.

I run over to the main control panel and flip it on. The lights flicker to life and their dim glow fills the small space. Faint static comes through the radio. I fiddle with the dial and try to adjust the volume, which only seems to make the static louder. I play with more knobs on the console until it clears and I hear a voice cut through. "—me?" I only catch the end of the transmission. Then it repeats and I catch the whole thing.

"Lucy, can you hear me?" It's Iris's voice, thank god.

"Yeah, what's going on?" I can hear the panic in my own voice.

"I managed to slip out through a side door, but the others got caught by the captain.

It probably won't be long before they catch me too," she says.

"How do I get back?" I ask.

"I'm afraid I don't have a way to bring you back. And even if I did, the ship is going to crash into that distortion in less than an hour." Through her words I manage to catch what she's implying, and the reality of my situation sinks in.

"It's got to be me, hasn't it?" I look out the shuttle window at the massive area of dark space.

"Lucy, I'm so sorry, if there was any other way, trust me, I wouldn't ask you to do this." I don't say anything as I let this decision sit with me. She's right, isn't she? I could go back but it would mean the ship gets destroyed. This is the right choice.

"No, this is how it should be," I say.

"I can walk you through what you're going to need to do," Iris says. I can tell she's trying to find the right balance of comfort and hurrying us along.

"Go ahead." I say.

"Well the first thing you're gonna need to do is initialize the warp unit," Iris says.

I start looking around the shuttle. "But isn't that for making space jumps?"

"It's gonna do a couple of things for you," Iris responds. "Do you see a large blue button above you?"

I look up and see the button above the console. "Yes, do you want me to push it?"

"NO!" she shouts quickly. I move my hand away from the button. "That button will activate the warp unit and open a rift in space. You should not use that until you are inside the space distortion. And before that, we have to initialize the drive to protect the shuttle. Do you see a small silver switch next to it?"

"Yes." I don't try to reach for that one yet, just in case.

"Good. Go ahead and flip that switch, ok?"

Ok, I guess this one I do touch. I flip the switch and a blue light appears around the shuttle. "What did that do?"

"It's created a low-level warp field around your shuttle. That should allow you to fly directly into the spacial distortion," she explains.

"Why couldn't we just have done that for the whole ship?" I ask.

"Because this ship is massive. There's just not enough energy to generate a warp field around something this big for that long. Not without also having the warp drive running at full power, which could've sent us right into the distortion," she responds.

"So now what?"

"Now you will need to pilot the shuttle towards the big distortion," she says.

"How do I know exactly where it is?" I look out at the vague dark areas of space ahead of me. It all kind of blends together.

"I found a way to access the readouts we set up in the observatory from here. I can help guide you around them," she says. I place my hands on the wheel. "Fly forward and get clear of the ship." I push the wheel forward and feel the shuttle start to move further away from the ship. "Good, now turn the shuttle left," she says, and I do so, following along the hull. "Good, you're doing great. Just keep following the hull."

The shuttle glides along smoothly. The ship's hull beneath me looks so cold and metal, such a stark contrast from the warmth and life of the decks inside. It's such a different perspective seeing it from out in space like this.

"While you're doing that, I need to tell you a few more things," Iris chimes in. "When you enter the space distortion, I'm probably going to lose contact with you. So I need to make sure you know all of the important stuff now," she explains.

"Ok, I'm listening," I say.

"From the instant you enter the distortion, you're going to wait exactly thirty-four seconds before activating the warp unit. That should ensure that you're as close to the center as you can get."

"Thirty-four seconds. Got it." I nod.

"Adjust your heading twenty degrees up," she says.

"Wait, twenty degrees?"

There's a sigh. "Pull the wheel up a little." I pull back on the wheel and the shuttle adjusts upwards. I can see the end of the ship now.

"Is that all?" I ask.

"No, there's one more thing. We took the long-range scanners from the observatory and put them into the shuttle. Masumi rigged up a beacon in the observatory so you can locate us if you drift apart from the *Mercury*. As long as you can pick up our signal, the AI in the shuttle should be able to help you send us a message," Iris says. I watch as the shuttle floats past the bridge of the ship.

"Well, hopefully I won't end up too far away," I joke.

"Are you ready, Lucy?" Iris asks.

"I guess as much as I'll ever be," I tell her.

"You're about ten seconds away from the edge of the distortion," Iris says. I look out in front of the shuttle. The darkness feels close. No stars. Just emptiness and a sinking feeling deep in my gut.

"Good luck, Lucy," Iris says. "And we'll see you soo—" Her voice cuts off as the shuttle drifts past the edge of the distortion.

My jaw drops as the darkness of space disappears. Bright light and waves of color swirl around the exterior of the shuttle. A far cry from the dark empty void that I was expecting. It's a surreal landscape of color and undefinable shapes. I begin counting in my head. One, two, three. There is no sound. Everything is silent and brilliant.

I can feel the movement of the shuttle as I watch the space and colors distort around me. Eleven, twelve, thirteen. Every second I think I see a familiar shape outside the window but before my brain can process it, it's already shifted into something else entirely. I wonder if this is what Atticus saw in his last moments. Hopefully, it won't be what I see in mine.

The colors around me get brighter as the seconds pass. They are becoming less defined, blending together until it's nothing more than a bright light. Twenty-three, twenty-four, twenty-five. I see more glimpses of things around me. Or possibly places? Or just tricks of the light? I see what looks like my own shuttle outside the window. It could also just be a reflection. Then suddenly I see something truly spectacular.

It's a massive city, bigger than the entire *Mercury*, with spires and monuments stretching out far above me. And it seems to hang, floating in this mysterious bright landscape like an island. What could that possibly be? Twenty-nine, thirty, thirty-one. I reach up from the chair and place my hand on the blue button. Thirty-two, thirty-three, thirty-four.

I press the button.

The colors around the shuttle are suddenly drowned out by a piercing blue light that envelops everything. The silence from before is cut by a loud ringing, echoing through my head and causing a sharp pain. I place my head in my hands and suddenly the blue light vanishes and the ringing stops.

Outside the shuttle, the bright landscape and swirls of color are gone, leaving only darkness. But as my eyes start to adjust, I see tiny specks of light all around me. Stars. I'm back in normal space. Could that have actually worked? I look all around the shuttle and find there's not a single patch of darkness left. But my heart sinks when I realize what else is no longer there. I look out in all directions again just to be sure but, unfortunately, it seems to be true.

The *Mercury* is gone.

CHAPTER TWELVE

DRIFTING

The shuttle spins around as I tilt the wheel back and forth but the result is the same in every direction; nothing but emptiness. What am I supposed to do now? I think back to what Atticus had said about the warp drive. He said it opened up a hole from one part of space to another, right? Is that what happened here? And if that is what happened, where did I end up?

I step away from the controls and look around the cabin but find that it's pretty sparse. It might have looked nice at one point, but any of that niceness was stripped away by Egon and Nao when they prepped the shuttle. There are even some odd scraps of metal scattered across the floor that they likely didn't have time to clean up.

I walk back over to the pilot's chair and slump down into it. My eyes drift up to the control panel with its lights still blinking brightly every few seconds. I look down at the console in front of me and examine all the buttons. I hadn't really had the chance to earlier, but I do see one with a microphone icon on it.

"Hello?" I say loudly as I press down the microphone button. "Are you there, *Mercury*? I'm having a little bit of trouble seeing your location." I wait a couple of seconds before trying again. "Iris?" There's still no response, just empty static. I take my finger off the button and the static cuts out, leaving silence again. I lean back in the chair.

What happened to everyone after the captain and Helena caught them? I feel bad I didn't get to say a proper goodbye. Although, I guess I also didn't say bye to anyone in my time either. From their perspective, it probably looks like I just disappeared.

I've been so swept up in the chaos of the space distortions it's actually been a while since I've thought about my time, or more importantly, how I'm supposed to get back there. Although right now I'd settle for just getting back to the *Mercury*. Assuming the ship didn't get destroyed by the space distortions. I mean, I'm here, right? And logically since the ship was still there in my time it must've worked. But there's still a pit in my stomach. I put my feet up on the console in front of me and accidentally press another button.

"Do you require assistance?" a voice asks from the other side of the shuttle, nearly causing me to fall out of my chair. I whip around and look at the empty space, still a little disoriented from my train of thought being so abruptly derailed.

"Who's there?" I ask.

"This is your AI pilot, WILEY. Is there anything I can assist you with?" I walk over to a panel on the opposite side of the room showing a small, pixelated face on the screen. This must be the shuttle's AI that Iris mentioned.

"Oh, it's you," I say. The only thing worse than drifting alone in space is drifting in space with an annoying AI unit.

"Do you require assistance?" it asks again in a chipper tone. They never really figured out how to make an AI that could read the room, did they?

"No. I'm just trying to work out how I can get out of this mess," I say.

"May I ask what mess you are trying to clean up?"

"Not a literal mess. Like, I'm stuck in the middle of space in this shuttle," I explain.

"Where would you like to go?" it asks.

"Back to the *Mercury*," I tell it. "But it's not anywhere nearby."

"Would you like to scan for a signal?"

"Yeah, why not."

"Scanning for signals," it says. The shuttle echoes with a couple of beeps and a few pings before falling silent again. "Close range scanners appear to be offline. No readings could be completed at this time."

"You're a huge help," I say sarcastically.

"Happy to be of assistance!" it chirps before turning itself off. The AI units have never been very good at recognizing sarcasm either. I guess that's a good thing, though. They'd probably turn against us if they ever realized how mean we actually are to them.

I walk back toward the front of the shuttle and stretch my legs. There's a subtle blue light pulsing around the outside of the shuttle as I look out the windows. So that's the warp bubble. I walk over to the console, flip the switch off again, and watch the blue light slowly fade as the humming of the warp core disappears. The shuttle feels even quieter than before.

I continue pacing around and start to take stock of everything. I mean, I've still got power, which is good, there's the radio and deep space scanners, the shuttle thrusters still seem to work, and, of course, there's the warp core. Although I don't know what good it'll do me now.

I pull open a small door on the wall to find an old matter replicator inside. It looks like it's even still got a few printing blocks left, which will help with food or supplies for a while. There's a small locker on the same wall with an old spacesuit inside. I pull open another small door to find the world's smallest bathroom. On the opposite wall, there's a small handle near the floor. I walk over and tug on it. A small panel drops down and slams loudly on the floor, revealing a tiny, uncomfortable-looking cot.

Guess that's about all I've got here. Content with my inventory, I sit back down at the helm and tap on the console. The systems read out on a small screen as I scroll through them. LIFE SUPPORT — 108 HOURS. That's like, what, four days? RESERVE BACKUP POWER SYSTEM NOT FOUND. Egon and Nao must've taken that out when they were prepping the shuttle.

I sit and think about my next course of action, but the thinking doesn't get me very far. It doesn't feel like there's anything I can do to help this situation. Maybe if I at least knew where I was I'd feel a bit better about it.

"WILEY, can you tell me what part of space I'm in?"

WILEY chimes back on. "Certainly! You are in sector Z291-O3," it says. Complete gibberish.

"And how far are we from the previously known location of the *Mercury*?"

"We are currently one mile from the pre-vious location of the *Mercury*," it responds. I pause and process what it just said.

"Wait, what? One mile? That can't possi-bly be right," I demand.

"According to the star charts, we have not traveled any distance greater than one mile from our original destination."

"The spacial distortions must have thrown you off," I tell it.

"That is incorrect. There has been no in-ternal error with my navigational systems," it assures me.

"Then if we haven't moved, where is the *Mercury*?"

"Insufficient data," it responds. I look out the window again. What exactly happened in that space distortion?

I had assumed it threw me to some other corner of space but what if it wasn't me that got moved, but actually the *Mercury*? Not that that makes things any easier since I could still be thousands of miles away from where the *Mercury* is now. Or, for all I know, the *Mercury* could still have hit the space distortion and been destroyed.

"WILEY, can you perform a long-range scan looking for the *Mercury*?" I ask.

"Long-range scan initiated. Estimated time until finish, thirty-four hours."

Great, what am I supposed to do for that long? As the thought of waiting for the results of this scan sinks in, I suddenly realize how exhausted I am. By my guess, I've probably been awake for almost a full day at this point.

I walk over to the cot and lay down across it. It's stiff and uncomfortable but at least it's something, right? I look up at the metal ceiling of the shuttle and drift off to sleep.

◆

I find myself walking in a place I've never been before. Massive buildings tower on either side of me, taller than any I've ever seen on the *Mercury*. I look up but there's no deck above me. Everything seems to be painted in a deep blue glow. I keep walking, the street continuing for what feels like an eternity until I eventually reach the end. But not just any end, the street seems to stop out of nowhere and then drop down like a cliff. I look over the edge and see a landscape thousands of miles below. In the distance is another city floating through the clouds and I realize where I've seen this before. This is what I saw while I was in that distortion. How did I end up back here, though?

I blink and suddenly I'm somewhere completely different. It looks exactly like the

forest back on the *Mercury*, even smells the
same, but I can tell it's different somehow. I
walk forward into a small clearing where
there's a crater filled to the brim with glowing
blue flowers, they seem to glow brighter as I
run my fingers through them. I've seen these
before—

The scene changes again and I'm floating
above the hull of the *Mercury*. Is it possible?
Did I make it back? I look down and see three
figures standing on the hull in spacesuits.
Wait. I look down at my feet to find myself
standing on a glowing blue crystal. That's
when it clicks, this is the meteor we saw. And
sure enough, I look back at the figures again
and recognize them as Atticus, Helena, and
myself. I can't figure out what's going on—

BEEP BEEP BEEP

I'm suddenly jolted awake by a loud
alarm ringing through the shuttle. It was just a
dream? It felt so real.

"WILEY! What's that alarm?" I shout.

"Life support has fallen to ninety-six
hours remaining," the mechanical voice responds.

"Turn it off."

"Alarm has been silenced." I still feel a
little disoriented from the abrupt awakening. I
roll onto my back and stare at the ceiling.

"Why'd it go off, anyways?" I ask.

"The alarm is programmed to alert shuttle inhabitants when life support functions are lowering."

"Ok, well you can go ahead and stop that. I'm very aware of how long I've got left," I tell it. I pull myself up from the cot, my joints cracking loudly as I do. It was definitely not the most comfortable place to sleep but at least I slept like a rock. My stomach growls as I wake up more.

I walk over to the matter replicator and turn it on, reading through the list of options that pop up on the screen. I pick the one that says FOOD and a giant list scrolls across the screen. Usually, despite the staggering array of options, every time I use one of these replicators I get a food block that only vaguely resembles the taste of what I actually wanted.

I tap the option that reads 'BLUEBERRY PANCAKES' and the machine whirrs to life. It produces a lot of noise considering it's just making a brick with a bit of flavoring in it, but I sit back and wait for it anyways. About two minutes later there's a small chime letting me know that it's finished. I slide open the metal door and much to my surprise there's an actual meal inside instead of a brick.

The smell of the pancakes fills the entire room. Not only did it deliver the food on a beautiful fancy plate, but it also printed a

matching knife and fork. I transfer the plate to
my lap and dig in, the pancakes melting in my
mouth. The blueberries taste like the ones I
used to pick down on the ship's farms as a
kid. I've got to hand it to this replicator, it
really nailed the food. And hey, at least if I'm
going to die out here, I'll die well-fed.

I continue to devour the pancakes as I
listen to the pings from Wiley's deep-space
scans. "How's it going over there WILEY?" I
ask, my mouth full of pancakes.

"The deep space scan is thirty-seven percent complete," it responds. I guess I've got a
little more time to kill. I look around the cabin but there's not really anything else to do in
here. I finish the pancakes and place the plate
next to the bed before going over to the helm
again. I slump down into the chair and listen
to the pinging of the scanner.

◆

I see Atticus. He's standing in the cafeteria again, looking up at the ceiling. He turns
and looks at me directly, holding the radio up
to his mouth. I watch his lips move but I can't
make out what he says. Then the ceiling rips
open and he's thrown into space.

Then I see him in the cafeteria again. He
looks at me and raises the radio to his mouth,

saying something final into it. Then he's tossed out into space again.

And just as before, I'm back at the start. Standing there looking at Atticus, watching the same scene play out over and over.

I wake up in a cold sweat. Damn it, another dream. Or rather, a nightmare. That's definitely not a moment I want to relive anytime soon. There's a pit in my stomach just thinking about it.

I head over to the matter synthesizer and scroll through until I see what I'm looking for. I press the screen and it flashes 'ICE CREAM'. I close the door and it whirrs away.

I've only ever heard of ice cream in books. I never thought I'd get the chance to actually try some. After a minute, the machine chimes and I slide open the door. As my hand touches the metal the temperature difference is considerable, even colder than when I held the warp core. A wave of cold air comes out of the small compartment. Inside is a small glass bowl filled with a grouping of cream-colored balls. There's a matching glass spoon sitting on the brim of the bowl.

I take the cold bowl out of the replicator, grab the crystal spoon, and scoop out a bit of the stuff inside, raising it to my lips. The flavor and consistency are unlike anything I've ever tasted before. The cold texture melts against my tongue. This is probably the best replicator I've ever come across for making food. I wonder if there are any on the ship that are as good as this one.

I shovel more of the ice cream into my mouth. I eat quickly until there is a sharp pain at the front of my head. It seems to come out of nowhere. I try to finish the last of the ice cream but that only makes it worse. I look around the room but everything appears to be fine there. I see no source that would be causing me that kind of pain.

"WILEY, what's going on with the shuttle right now?" I ask.

"The deep space scan is currently at forty-one percent complete," it responds. I guess everything on the shuttle is fine. I put the bowl down. Oh no. Maybe it was the ice cream. Is my body not designed to eat food like that? Or, wait, that's also the first time I've eaten something that cold. Could that have done it? I put my head in my hands and slowly feel the pain fade away. I relax slightly. Whatever it was seems to be passing. That was certainly weird.

I put the bowl down on top of the plate from the pancakes and they clatter together loudly. I scroll through the rest of the options on the synthesizer menu. There's a whole section for tools, another for books, but none of these really jump out at me. Plus, it would probably be best to save the last prints in the

machine for food. Although in another few
days when the life support runs out I guess it
won't really matter how much I've printed.

I spend the next few hours scrolling
through the shuttle's systems, trying to see if
there's anything useful in them. A couple
more hours staring out into space. But finally,
I decide to get some sleep again. I lay down
on the cot and try to tune out the thoughts I'm
having about dying alone in space. But without anything to distract me, the thoughts flood
into my head. Tears run down my face as I
finally drift off to sleep.

✦

I'm back in the brig again. Or is it the
Proscenium? I guess they're kind of the same.
A hologram of my mom appears onstage. It's
the brig, then. Although this time she's not in
her regular white uniform like I'm used to.
No, she's in a fancy evening gown, her hair
long and flowing over her shoulders.

That's when I realize it's not a hologram,
it's a spotlight. She starts singing and the
crowd around me cheers for her. I turn to look
at the person sitting next to me and see Helena, staring up at the stage with wide eyes.
Wait, how are there two of her?

I look back up onstage and see it's now
the younger Helena up there singing, wearing

the same dress that she wore when we went to the show together. I turn to look beside me and see my mother staring up at the stage with the same wide-eyed look that her younger self had had just a moment before. But then her expression changes and I watch as she bawls her eyes out.

Before I can process what's going on, I'm woken up by a new, loud pinging sound. I can feel tears rolling down my cheeks too.

"What's going on?" I ask.

"Deep Space Scan completed," WILEY says.

I drag myself over to the chair and look at the console in front of me. "What'd you find?"

"Scan identified two signals matching your criteria," it says.

"What do you mean two signals?"

"Two distinct signals are being picked up by our equipment," it says again.

"Well, which one is the ship?"

"Insufficient data to determine."

"One of them has to be the *Mercury*, right? But what could the other one be?" I ask.

"Insufficient—"

"Yeah, you've already said that. Do you know what else could make a signal like that out here?" I try asking.

"Insufficient data to determine." Wow, that's becoming a really annoying answer.

"How close are they to each other?"

"The first signal is originating from a heading of 37-29-83 at a distance of two light years away. The second signal is originating at 230-29-51 at a distance of three light years away," it explains. More space gibberish.

"Yeah, but are they close to each other? Or far away?" I ask.

"That is correct."

I take a deep breath and remind myself I can't destroy the AI. "Which one is correct?"

"The two signals originate in opposite directions from our current position."

"Well, that's not super helpful, is it? How long would it take us to get to either of those signal locations?"

"Under the power of this shuttle it would take approximately forty-four thousand years to reach the first signal and sixty-six thousand years to reach the second signal," it says.

"We'll keep that as a backup option," I say. What else could we use to get there? And on top of that, which signal do I even want to get to? Iris said Masumi rigged the beacon into the observatory of the *Mercury*, right? So that has to be one of them. But I'm still stumped about what that other signal could be. Maybe it's another ship. No matter what, though, I still don't have a way to get there. Then it suddenly occurs to me...

"What about the warp unit?" I ask.

"To what are you referring?"

"The warp unit that we wired into the shuttle! Could that get me to one of those signals?" I ask. There is a pause.

"It is not an advisable course of action," it warns.

"Oh yeah? And why not?"

"The warp unit installed in this shuttle is designed to be activated and generate a warp field in a stationary location. It is not integrated into the navigational systems of this shuttle," it explains.

"What does that mean?"

"You would be able to activate the warp unit, however without navigation there is no way to navigate once the jump has been initiated. There will also be no visibility to our destination," it continues.

"Maybe I'm just not getting what you're saying," I say.

"Without navigation, there is a forty-seven percent chance that we will crash into something during the warp jump. Once the jump is initiated it will not cease until we either arrive at the destination or the shuttle is destroyed. There is no data to determine the likelihood that a shuttle like this will be able to survive a warp jump at all," it finishes.

Forty-seven percent, huh? All things considered, those sound like the best odds I've heard all day. "Can you make sure we're pointed in the exact right direction?" I ask.

"Yes, my navigational systems are integrated with all the shuttle's native thrusters."

Good. That's going to be super helpful. "Is there anything we can do to help with that forty-seven percent chance of crashing into something?"

"There is not," it responds.

"I feel like that can't be true."

"It is my accurate assessment," it says.

Another thought crosses my mind. "What about if we put the warp field on again?"

"Insufficient data to make a determination." Ok, that's it. I'm deciding how we do this now.

"You know what, I'm done asking you questions. We've got to do something here." I walk over and flip on the warp field switch. The blue light surrounds the shuttle again. Perfect. Who knows if it'll help but it's worth a shot, right?

"You said there's no way to tell which of the signals is the right one?" I ask.

"That is correct," WILEY responds.

"Then pick one at random and point me towards it. If it's not right we'll give the other one a shot," I say. The shuttle begins to spin around in place until we're facing a new di-

rection. "So what do we need to do to make
the jump?"

"Press the warp button," WILEY says.
Simple enough, I guess. "But I would advise
securing yourself in the pilot's seat first.
There is no data to show what will happen
when this shuttle generates a warp field. You
should prepare for a rough journey," it says.
Probably smart.

"You know, you're not very optimistic for
AI," I tell it. It does not respond. Oh well. I
run over to the locker, get out the old spacesuit, and quickly pull it on. This one feels a
lot bulkier and less flexible than some of the
others I've worn. I sit down in the pilot's seat
and pull the straps around the suit, buckling
myself into place.

"I guess there's only one thing left to do,"
I say as I reach up to the blue button. I gently
press it and the entire ship drops out of space.

My body suddenly feels like it's being
stretched out of shape and yet at the same
time it feels like I've just fallen off a cliff. I
open my eyes to look outside and the world
around me is nothing more than a blur and a
glow of bright blue light. Inside the shuttle,
everything behind me is stretched out beyond
recognition. I can hear deep, distorted noises,
but I can't identify what's making them. I try
to breathe but no air reaches my lungs while

at the same time it feels like space is closing in around me.

After what feels like hours, there's a sound that nearly ruptures my ears. The blue light vanishes and I'm thrown into darkness. Everything snaps back into its proper proportions and falls completely silent.

My consciousness starts to slip away.

◆

I wake up suddenly and reach up to feel my face, but the helmet stops my hands. I must have passed out but luckily I'm still in one piece. None of the lights of the shuttle are working anymore, just the dim light coming from my helmet. The walls are crumpled inwards and I can't even tell where the main window used to be. Everything is just a twisted heap of metal.

Then, from deep inside the core of the shuttle, a blue light starts emitting, bleeding through all the cracks in the metal. I hear a noise from outside and a large singular pulse emits from the warp unit. There is a loud crack like thunder and then silence again. I look around but there doesn't seem to be any way out. And from the state the shuttle is in right now, I get the sinking feeling that this is the only jump it's going to make. I hope that I

picked the right signal to follow. And if I
didn't, then where did this jump take me?

CHAPTER THIRTEEN

HELENA

The shuttle feels way more claustrophobic with the walls folded inwards. They look like crumpled-up pieces of paper except for being jagged and metal. The suit's helmet is black and charred, not enough to fully block out my vision, but just enough to make it super hard to see anything too clearly. I fumble around with the buckles and finally manage to release the straps from the pilot's chair.

I walk around and take in the destroyed shuttle. It almost sounds like there's a faint noise coming from outside but nothing clear enough for me to actually make out. I feel around the walls, avoiding the sharper edges, and try to locate the shuttle door. But with everything twisted together, it's almost impossible to tell where it used to be.

Something crunches under my boot and I look down. It's glass. Where could that possibly have come from? Is it the front window? Oh my god no, it's the glass ice cream bowl.

It looks like both it and the ornate plate didn't fare too well during that warp jump. I also notice one of the metal floor panels has peeled back a little bit. I reach down and try to open it further but it doesn't want to budge.

I stand back up and give the panel a firm kick, which seems to loosen it considerably. I try pulling it up again, finally managing to separate it from the floor of the ship. It reveals a small compartment of tools I totally missed when I was looking around the shuttle earlier.

I rifle through the compartment until I find something somewhat useful — a welding arc. It's smaller than I would've preferred but it's better than nothing. I look up at the wall of the shuttle with the welding arc in hand. Cutting through that's going to be a little like trying to fill a fountain with a teacup. Nonetheless, it's all I've got. I check my suit first; I've got no idea if there's even a safe atmosphere outside. For all I know, I could be on some random planet.

I start cutting into the wall and I feel the resistance almost immediately. The wall is thick and certainly not meant to be cut through like this. Hell, it survived a full crash at warp speed. Anything that can handle that must be pretty resilient.

I work slowly, slicing away back and forth at angles, trying to carve my way deeper

into the hull. Large chunks of metal clatter to the ground as I work. The welding arc doesn't seem to reach all the way through, but I push ahead anyway. I'm sure any experienced shipbuilder would laugh at my technique but luckily I don't have an audience for my rough cutting. The welding arc is heavy in my arms and after a couple more minutes I power it down to rest.

The wall has a faint criss-cross glow from where I've been slicing and the chunks of metal on the floor have the same glow, now starting to fade. I wonder how much longer it's going to take as my stomach growls. Maybe I should've eaten something more substantial than pancakes and ice cream when I had the chance.

After I've rested for a few minutes and regained some energy, I get up and power on the welding arc again. I continue slicing until I finally see a small hole of light shining through. A burst of air rushes into the shuttle. That must mean wherever I am has an atmosphere, right? That's good at least.

I dig the welding arc into the wall around the light and slowly start to carve out a larger circle, the metal now falling outwards instead of inwards. After another few minutes, I've managed to cut away a section that looks big enough for me to squeeze through with the suit on. The light pouring in is bright enough that I can barely make out any details of what's outside, but there are definitely noises. I power down the welding arc and set it on the floor.

Then I look around the shuttle one last time before starting to climb out of the hole. I go slowly and carefully, feeling around for some kind of outside surface. I reach my foot down and it connects with something. When I slowly put my weight onto it, whatever it is seems to hold up. The surface is smooth with ridges along it and luckily nothing catches on the suit. I step fully out of the shuttle onto this new ground and my eyes start to adjust to the bright light.

I hear a noise from behind and turn to look. Figures surround me. I can't make out their details through my charred visor but I can tell they're getting closer. I try to hide up against the side of the shuttle before quickly realizing that that won't work. They've clearly already seen me.

The figures move closer and I try to scramble back into the shuttle. I get about halfway inside before something firmly grasps my foot and pulls me back out. The figures throw me to the ground. This new place doesn't seem to be the most welcoming.

I struggle to break free, but the figures have me pinned. A sharp pinch stings my neck and a sudden drowsiness sets in. I make one last attempt to break free but it does no good as my eyes close and my consciousness slowly drifts away.

✦

I jolt awake and immediately panic when I notice my spacesuit is gone. I sit up and look around to find myself in a small metal room lying on a bed. I attempt to get up and nearly pull my arm out of its socket, not realizing that it's handcuffed to the bed. The handcuffs dig painfully into my wrist. I sit back down and look around the room.

There are almost no discernible features here. Plain metal walls, floor, and ceiling, with a tiny cot in the corner. There's a part of the wall that looks like it could be the door, but I can't be sure since it doesn't have any kind of handle. There's a dim flickering light on the ceiling that's making an annoying humming noise. I twist my wrist and slip out of the handcuffs.

For the moment I seem to be safe, but I start looking for possible ways out, just to be on the safe side. As I'm doing this, the door swings outwards and a man walks in wearing a deep green uniform. I recognize it instantly as the security officer's uniform.

"Wait, I'm back on the *Mercury*?" I feel a wave of relief wash over me. I can't believe I'm actually back.

The officer stops and looks at me with confusion. "You're familiar with our ship?"

"What are you talking about? Of course I am," I say.

He looks even more confused as he holds a clipboard, tapping it impatiently. "Where did you come from?"

"That's a bit of a long story," I say.

"Then start talking."

"Well, I flew one of the shuttles out to save the ship from the space distortions," I say.

His eyes narrow. "What space distortions?"

"What do you mean 'what space distortions'? The whole ship was about to be torn apart," I say.

"You're not making any sense," he says. Nothing I say in this conversation seems to be going very well.

"It's the truth." How could he not know about those? I mean, the whole ship was about to start disembarkment. That's kind of a hard thing to miss.

"We'll let the captain be the judge of that. She's on her way down," he says before walking back over to the door. He pulls it shut as he leaves. I think back to my last interaction with the captain and how poorly it had gone. I remember her standing there screaming at us in the shuttle bay before we went completely rogue and launched the shuttle.

I sit in the room for another couple of minutes, my sense of dread building. I mean, she seems like a reasonable person, but I also have no idea how long she's likely to hold a grudge. Hopefully it's less time than I was out in the shuttle for, otherwise I feel like I'm going to be in a lot of trouble.

I hear voices on the other side of the door before it swings open again. Although instead of the captain stepping through, it's my mother. Not Helena, my mother from back in my time. Same wrinkles on her face and stern expression. And those cold eyes.

"You've got some serious explaining to do here," she says. I'm at a total loss for words. Where is my grandmother? Isn't she the captain?

"What's going on?" I ask.

"What's going on is that you're going to explain exactly what you were doing climbing around that meteor," she says.

I try to piece together what she's talking about, but I'm completely lost. "What meteor?"

"The one we caught you climbing out of!" Her voice gets louder.

"You mean the shuttle?"

"No, I mean the meteor that just crashed into the ship," she says, and my brain finally starts to put the pieces together. Whatever I did with those space distortions must have brought me back to my own time. So that meteor that crashed into the *Mercury* wasn't a meteor at all, it was my shuttle. I look back up at my mom. It's really her, just like she was before I left.

I have to tell her, I know I do, I just have to find the right thing to say. Maybe this time I can finally get through to her. "Do you remember the space distortions that almost destroyed the ship?" I ask her. "It would be twenty-one years ago for you, but you must remember."

"How do you know about those?" She masks it but I can see the surprise on her face.

"Because I was there." Best to just jump right into it.

She scoffs. "That's impossible."

"We knew each other back then," I say. "We spent almost two weeks together."

Her brow creases for a moment. "Lucy, please, I've had enough of your games and your wild stories," she says, but I can tell there was a small part of her that believed me. Even if she doesn't realize it yet.

"We went to see a show at the Proscenium," I continue. "You leant me that green jumpsuit, which looked great on me by the way so you better still have it in your closet."

She turns away. "I don't have time to listen to—"

"We watched the meteor on the side of the ship, hung out together in the observatory and had dinner in your quarters with your friends." I stand up and walk over to her, determined to finally get through. "You made cookies and introduced me to peanut butter because we don't have it in this time."

"Lucy, stop!" she yells, spinning back around to face me. "I don't know what you're playing at or how you know about that girl, but how dare you dredge up such horrible memories. She died that day in those distortions, just like your father."

"That's not true! It was me in that shuttle!" I protest. "I was the girl. That's how I know all of this. Think about it, how else could I possibly have found out?"

She shakes her head, and she actually seems speechless, as if she's starting to realize I'm telling the truth. "I don't see how that's possible."

"After our last conversation in the Proscenium, I went to check on the meteor," I explain, and hold my hand up before she can cut in. "I know I shouldn't have, and you can tell me off for it later, but let me finish. When I touched it, I don't know how, but it sent me back twenty-one years. Grandmother was the captain, and she put you in charge of looking after me. That's how we ended up meeting."

Her mouth hangs open slightly, and I can tell she's remembering it, the day we met in the brig. "I don't understand."

"I'm still putting it all together myself," I assure her.

She shakes her head again, as if she's trying to shake off the reality setting in on her. "Ok, fine, let's say I believe you for a minute. I can't begin to deal with all of that right now. None of this is particularly relevant to our current predicament." Back to business as usual.

My heart sinks a little. I was so close. "What predicament?"

"When the meteor, or shuttle or whatever it was, crashed into the ship we lost a number of our systems. We managed to fix the hole in the side of the ship, but our systems are beginning to shut down all over the *Mercury*," she explains.

"How long until they're fixed?"

"Not all of them can be. Not this time. We've lost dozens of essential life support systems. Those were designed to never fail, but it turns out being tunneled through with a thousand-ton shuttle is enough to shut them down."

"So, what does that mean?"

She sighs heavily. "We're gonna lose fresh water and air within a few weeks. Food will probably run out even sooner." I recognize that same tone in her voice. Just like when Atticus died; she sounds completely defeated.

"What're you gonna do about it?"

"There's not really anything we can do. We're just going to have to make everyone as comfortable as possible for the remaining time," she says. I can't believe the words that are coming out of her mouth. "Now, if you'll excuse me, I've got a lot left to deal with here."

Something inside me finally snaps. "NO," I shout as she goes to leave. We can't keep doing this. I'm not gonna let her give up that easily.

"What do you mean 'no'?" She turns back to me. "What do you want from me, Lucy?" And that's when I can see it clearly, the pain behind those cold eyes.

"I want to talk!" I say forcefully.

"I don't have time to talk right now. I just told you—"

"Why do you hate me so much?" I feel a lump in my throat, but I push it down.

She shakes her head and tries to brush me off again. "This really isn't the best time for this."

"No, we're doing this now. I want to hear why you can't stand to be around me." I can hear the anger in my voice. Of the two of us, it's not normally me who gets mad, but I've hit my limit. I'm done with her avoiding this conversation. After everything I just went through, it's time we get this out in the open.

"Lucy—"

"I know it's not just because you're busy with work. You go out of your way to avoid me."

"That's not true," she says.

"It absolutely is!" I say, holding back the tears. "What is it about me that you can't stand to be around?"

"Because you're just like him!" she yells back. Her words hang in the air between us.

"What?"

"Every time I look in your eyes, I see him looking back at me. I do love you, Lucy, but every time I look at you it breaks my heart all over again." There it is, the truth. The tears are rolling down her face.

"I can wear goggles if that would help," I make a poorly-timed joke and she gives out a little chuckle through the tears.

"It's not just the eyes. You're really just like him in so many ways, even the same bad jokes," she says.

"I'm sorry." I don't know what else to say.

"It's not your fault," she says with a sigh. The tears I had been holding back start to flow. I feel like part of me really needed to hear her say that. I cry and neither of us says anything for a little bit. I finally manage to compose myself.

"I got to meet him," I say.

I see the realization on her face. "Yes, I suppose you did."

"I told him who I was, too," I say. "When we were finding a way to remove the warp core. Right before he…" I stop. I can't even bring myself to say it.

"So he knew…" she says.

"I think that's why he did it."

She raises an eyebrow. "Did what?"

"Closed the bulkhead. It wasn't just to make sure the warp core got back. He did it to save the two of us." I can see her think about that for a few seconds.

"Yes, I suppose he did…" There are another few moments of silence between us.

"He wouldn't like how things are with us," I say.

Her eyes soften a little. "No, you're probably right about that."

"You know, he wasn't the only one I got to meet," I say.

"Oh? Who else?" Clearly not everything has clicked together for her yet.

"Well, you," I say.

"Oh, right…"

"You were pretty different back then."

She looks away. "I was young."

"I had fun with you, though."

A small smile crosses her face. "Yeah, I guess I was pretty similar to you at that age." She looks back up at me. It's subtle, but that look behind her eyes is changing.

"The Proscenium was pretty cool. What happened to it?" I ask, thinking back to the show we went to see there.

She shakes her head. "You know, when I became the captain, I had to give up on a lot of things I wanted to do."

"Like being a singer?"

"Yeah. I suppose I shut it down because I was a little bitter about it." I can tell she regrets it. I remember the look on her face during that show. She was truly happy.

"I know you never really wanted to be the captain," I say.

"No, but it was my duty."

"But were you happy doing it?"

"Why wouldn't I be happy? It was my job." She sounds like she's trying to convince herself more than me.

"You know I don't want to be the first officer." I've wanted to tell her that for so long. It feels so good to finally get the words out.

"You're the captain's daughter! My daughter! It's your duty to take it over, just like I did," she says, slipping back into her stern tone of voice.

"I'll never be happy doing it! Wouldn't you rather I find something that I actually enjoy? Some kind of passion?" I see her consider it for a second before shaking it off.

"But that's not how the world works. Everyone has a pre-determined job," she says.

"Who says it has to be that way?"

"Lucy that's—"

"No, I'm breaking this cycle here." I take her hand in mine. "And I want you to do the same. You should give up the captain's chair."

She laughs loudly. "What? Give it up? And do what?"

"Become a singer. Just like you always wanted to!"

She pulls her hand away. "I'm afraid that's just not possible. The ship needs a captain." She pauses. "And it's too late to try now," she says a little quieter. There it is. I can feel how much she wants to be something else.

"What about Atticus?"

This one catches her off guard. "What about him?"

"Don't you think he would want you to be happy?"

"Lucy, this is so much bigger than that. And what would happen if I just gave up being captain? Especially with the ship falling apart."

"But—"

She raises her hand and stops me mid-sentence. "Although… I suppose if you didn't want to be the first officer anymore, we could have a conversation about it." She gives me a small smile and I see her again — Helena. Just a glimmer but I can feel some of the Helena I met starting to come back.

"Really? I don't have to do it?"

"That's not what I said. I said we could talk about it," she clarifies. Still, that's more progress than we've ever made.

"Thanks…" I pause before the next word, "Mom." I think that's the first time I've called her 'mom' in a really long time. She smiles again before a serious look overtakes her face once more.

"I'm afraid I really do have to go deal with the ship's life support systems failing." She turns to leave but pauses in the doorway, looking back toward me. "Do you, uh, want to come with me this time?" She sounds a little awkward.

"Uh, yeah," I say awkwardly in return. I jump up and we leave the room together. I can't seem to stop from smiling. After all these years, I finally got through to her.

CHAPTER FOURTEEN

REUNION

My mom and I walk onto the bridge and the entire senior staff stand at attention. It's been years since I've been up here, but it doesn't look like it's changed at all.

"Can someone give me a status update?" she asks. One of the crew, whose name is on the tip of my tongue, steps forward.

"We checked the air filtration system and it's as bad as we suspected. The main processor was completely destroyed by the meteor," the woman says.

"And there's no chance to repair it?" my mom asks.

"Honestly, there's nothing left to repair. It was pretty much turned to dust when it got hit."

I can't help but feel responsible for what's going on right now. After all, it was my shuttle that destroyed all the systems. If I hadn't jumped, then the ship would still be intact. Although then the meteor wouldn't have been there to send me back in time in the first place. And I guess then the ship might've been destroyed by the distortions. My brain hurts trying to think about the time travel.

"Anyone have ideas?" My mom looks around the room.

Some of the crew glance around nervously before one finally steps forward. "Have we considered disembarkation?" He's another member of the senior crew but I can't seem to remember his name either. It's not like we really run in the same circles.

"I have thought about that. Believe me, more than you would know." She gives me a knowing look.

I decide to join in the conversation. "It's just a temporary solution. There aren't any planets nearby to disembark to." I look at my mom for confirmation and she gives me a nod. "And the shuttles also only have enough life support for a few weeks at most. Either way, the end result is the same whether everyone is in their shuttles or here on the *Mercury*."

My mom leans in with a smile. "You'd make a good first officer. Very authoritative," she whispers before turning back to the senior staff. "We'll keep that as an absolute last resort, but until we reach that point are there any other options to consider?"

"We haven't had engines on the *Mercury* for almost twenty years. It's not like we can really go anywhere," another crewperson chimes in. Their comment sparks an idea in my head.

"I think I have something," I say.

"What is it?" My mom looks at me. I can tell she's intrigued.

"What about the warp core?"

"The ship doesn't have a warp core anymore," she says. "We lost it when your shuttle flew into the space distortion." There's a beat before I see her put it together. "The shuttle that's sitting down on the biome deck." She smiles.

"The shuttle's destroyed but I think the warp core might've survived," I say.

She turns back to the crew with a determined look. "Ok, get an engineering crew down to that shuttle. We're going to take it apart piece by piece."

"What shuttle?" one of the crew asks.

"The meteor. It's a long story but it's actually an old survey shuttle from the ship. You're just going to have to trust me on this one." The crew nods and starts frantically radioing down to different parts of the ship.

"We're going to need help," I say to my mom.

She gestures around the room. "Why do you think I'm getting the engineering crews down there?"

"Not from them," I say, and she realizes who I'm talking about.

"No, I haven't spoken to any of them in twenty years," she argues.

"Tough. Because we need them today."

She looks away from me. "I let them all down, Lucy. I don't even know if they'll speak to me."

"Then let me do the talking," I say. She doesn't turn back to me but I can tell she's thinking about it. Finally, she sighs.

"Fine," she begrudgingly agrees.

"Good, now where's Iris?" I ask.

"She runs a small repair shop down on Deck Ten called Iris' Interstellar Inventions."

"Good, let's start there," I say.

The two of us make our way down to Deck Ten. Even with the chaos of everyone running around in a panic, the crowds still clear a path for my mom. We get even more stares than we did when she was just the first officer. I follow closely behind her, listening to the distinctive clang of her metal leg against the floor every other step. Now's probably not the time to bring up the fact that we both have a metal foot. Maybe that can be a fun surprise for later.

We walk along a street that feels familiar to me and as we get a little further down I realize why it looks so familiar. There's a shop that looks like it's been cobbled together from random junk and machine parts. Over the entrance sits a glowing neon sign in the shape of a purple flower. Wait, not just any flower... it's an iris...

"We're here," my mom says, stopping in front of the shop. It's the same one where that girl on the bike helped me out before. I can't seem to remember her name, though. What a crazy coincidence that I would end up back here.

"That's where Iris works?" I ask.

"Yes," she says.

I start walking towards the door but my mom stays where she is. "Aren't you coming in?" I ask her.

"I don't think I should, Lucy." She seems ashamed. It's not a look I've seen on her before. "I said some truly horrible things to her back then. Trust me, I think you'll probably have more luck without me." She's resolute in her decision not to join me so, begrudgingly, I continue up to the building without her. She's gonna have to see Iris at some point.

The metal door screeches like nails on a chalkboard as I pull it open. The interior of the shop looks about as cluttered and disorganized as the outside, and the entire room

smells like machine oil and smoke. Random objects are stacked on almost every surface and there's a low hum coming from somewhere in the room.

"Can I help you with something?" I hear a voice call from behind a stack of junk.

"I'm looking for Iris," I say. A person steps out from behind the stack. It's a young girl about my age. She has big round glasses and wild untamed hair that's been pulled back into a ponytail. Then it clicks.

"Penny," I say, finally remembering her name.

"Hey! Weird girl!" She looks me over for a couple of seconds and smiles. She leans in close to me and whispers. "Don't tell her about the bike, ok?" Then she stands up again and yells out into the shop, "Mom! Someone's here to see you!"

I hear rattling and a loud crash before another figure emerges from the back of the shop wearing a large pair of worn and cracked goggles that obscure most of their face. They pull off the old goggles and set them on the table nearby and while she's definitely older now, it's unmistakably Iris.

"Go check to see if any new orders have come in," she says to Penny before she walks towards me. Penny disappears into the back of the shop as Iris puts on a small pair of glasses.

"My name is—" I start as she's looking me over.

"Lucy," she cuts in.

"How did you know?"

She smiles. "You haven't aged a single day."

"Well, for me it's only been a few days since I've seen you," I say.

I can tell if I didn't already have her attention, this is what would've caught it. "What do you mean?"

"Whatever happened between that spacial distortion and the warp core somehow sent me back to my own time," I explain.

"Fascinating." Something about her feels different now. I can see the gears turning in her head as she processes this new information. When I met her before she always seemed to have boundless energy, asking endless questions, spewing off scientific theories, but I guess she's grown up a lot in the last twenty years.

"Do you know how that's even possible?" I ask.

"I'm afraid something like that is beyond even me. But the *Mercury* would've moved pretty far in the past twenty years. How did you find your way back to the ship?"

"I used the warp core to jump the shuttle."

"But how? I can't imagine you would've been able to navigate it very well," she says.

"Well, it's funny you mention that. I saw two signals and figured one must be the one Masumi set up in the observatory. And it turns out I was right."

When I mention Masumi's name, Iris' face changes. I can't pin down the emotion but whatever it was, it was definitely enough to get a reaction out of her. Then the emotion is replaced by one of realization when it all clicks together for her. "Wait, so the meteor that crashed into the ship…"

"Yeah, it was my shuttle," I say.

A big smile crosses her face and she gives me a very knowing look. "You used the warp bubble, didn't you?"

"How'd you know?"

"Well, you weren't flattened into a pan-cake is how I know." She laughs and I see a glimpse, if only for a second, of the Iris I knew. "But I am curious about something you just said. You mentioned you saw two sig-nals?"

"Yeah, I just picked one of them at ran-dom. Guess I got pretty lucky picking the right one," I say.

"Ok, the first signal was the *Mercury*, which makes total sense. But what the hell was the second one?" she asks. It's a valid question. And one that I considered heavily when I picked them up. Yet with all my theories about other ships, planets, or colonies I never actually found out what it was.

"I have no idea," I respond.

"Neither do I. And I don't like not knowing stuff." She picks up a bag from behind her worktable. "Let's go find that shuttle. I want to see if I can get the scanning equipment out of there and get to the bottom of this." Before I can fill her in on the state of the shuttle, she's already out the door. The second she's outside, she comes face to face with my mom and I can feel the tension. "Helena," Iris says.

"Long time no see, Iris," my mom says sheepishly.

"You could've visited."

"I didn't think you'd want to see me after what I said," she says.

"You weren't the only one who said things they regret that day." There's a long pause where neither of them says anything. I don't want to pry into their moment but I'm absolutely dying to know what happened between them after I left.

"I'm sorry," my mom says.

"Yeah, me too," Iris says.

Penny runs out of the shop after us. "Hey, what's going on?"

"Penny, this is Helena and Lucy. They're two very old friends of mine." Iris gives a smile.

"Nice to meet you, Penny." My mom reaches out her hand and Penny shakes it politely.

Iris leans down and puts her hand on Penny's shoulder. "We've got to go take care of something, but I'll be back later, ok?"

"Ok, I'll keep an eye on the shop," Penny says. She smiles at me again before running back inside.

"She's gotten so big," my mom says.

"Yeah, she's pretty incredible too," Iris says. "I heard the shuttle is back."

"That's why we came down to get you," my mom says. "We're going to reinstall the warp core back into the *Mercury*."

Iris thinks this over for a second, then nods. "Then you're going to need way more help than just me. Give me, like, ten minutes and I'll call the others. I'll tell everyone to meet us up on the biome deck where the shuttle crashed," she says.

I feel the hesitation radiating off of my mom. If she was this apprehensive about seeing Iris again, I can't imagine how she must be feeling about seeing the whole group back together. I try to think of something to say to comfort her as we make our way back to the bridleway but very little comes to mind. I mean, what could I possibly say to erase twenty years of baggage between them all?

Nevertheless, I attempt to make some small talk as we step into one of the chariots. "I think that went pretty well."

"I suppose so…" my mom says. She seems to be lost in thought, so I let the conversation fizzle out. I wish I knew how I could make her feel better but I'm realizing there's still so much about her that I don't know. We arrive on the biome deck and I'm greeted again by the smell of trees and smoke. We walk down the path towards the shuttle, finally arriving at the clearing.

There's a large crowd of engineers huddled around the shuttle, some cutting into it with large, glowing tools. Now, if I'd had one of those it would've made getting out of there way easier. They're careful with the cuts they make as they slowly expose more and more of the shuttle. After a few minutes of watching them work, Iris walks up behind us.

"How's the progress going?" she asks. I turn around and see Nao and Egon with her. Nao is wearing a white chef's coat and their head is completely shaved smooth like Masumi's used to be. Egon is wearing a pair of large overalls caked in a layer of dirt, very much like the ones he was wearing the last time I saw him. He's got an assortment of gardening tools hanging off his belt. The two look so much older now. I also get the sense

from their outfits that they were dragged
away from other jobs.

Egon's usually stoic face is broken by a
look of complete surprise. "Is that…Lucy?"

"Hey, Egon." I walk over and he lifts me
up in a big bear hug.

"We thought you were dead," Nao says.

"I always hoped you'd make it out somehow though," Egon adds, putting me back
down on the ground. He doesn't cry but I can
see his eyes are watery.

Nao also has a look of complete disbelief
on their face. Like they'd just seen a ghost.
"How did you make it out?"

"Look, we'll have time to catch up later,"
Iris cuts in.

"Is Masumi coming?" my mom asks. Nao
finally turns to her. At first, I had thought they
were just so excited to see me that they
missed that my mom was there too. But after
seeing the look on Nao's face, I realize they
were deliberately ignoring her.

"No, Helena. She didn't want to see you."
I can hear the bitterness in Nao's voice.

"Oh…" She sounds disappointed. Whatever went down with all of them must've
been pretty bad.

In her usual fashion, Iris steps in to quickly change the subject back to work. "Let's get
to the matter at hand."

"Yeah, what're we here for?" Nao asks Iris.

"For that." She points down to the shuttle.

"The meteor?" Egon asks.

"It's not a meteor," I say. "It's my shuttle. It crashed into the ship." They all look at me and then back to the shuttle before all at once rushing down into the crater for a closer look. My mom follows the group but hangs a little further back.

Nao looks over the wreckage with fascination. "Wow, Lucy, you really did a number on this one."

"It wasn't my fault!" I say. Everyone laughs.

"Ok, give me that." Iris grabs one of the cutting tools from a nearby engineer. She ducks down and climbs inside the shuttle as the rest of us follow her. She taps her foot around on the warped metal floor until she finds the spot she's looking for, then she abruptly digs the glowing blade into the floor, carving out a large circle. The metal melts underneath the blade and within seconds she's finished cutting. She kicks at the metal circle she just cut free. "Egon, can you get that panel up?"

"I think so." He pulls on a pair of thick leather gloves before reaching down to the loose panel. As he lifts it up, I see the glowing blue warp core inside. Somehow, despite everything that happened to me and the shuttle, the core doesn't seem to have a single scratch on it. Just the same blue light that it's always had filling the space around us.

"Grab that, Lucy," Iris says. I duck under the panel Egon is holding up and pull out the warp, core along with a tangled mess of cables attached to it.

"What're we going to do with—" but before I can ask about the cables and tubes, Iris has already sliced through, severing any connection they had to what remained of the shuttle. Egon drops the large panel back onto the floor.

"Ok, good. Lucy, you remember where that goes, right?" she asks.

I nod. "Of course."

"Good, you and Helena go get that reinstalled," she says.

I look around the room and realize my mom didn't follow us into the shuttle. "What about you?" I ask.

"The three of us are going to try and salvage the deep space scanners from the shuttle. I'm determined to figure out what that other signal you picked up is. Once you're done with that, come meet us on the bridge," Iris says.

I nod and step out of the shuttle to find my mom waiting outside awkwardly. "Why didn't you come inside?"

"Oh, come on, Lucy, they didn't want me there," she says.

"You know that's not true. You already patched things up with Iris. It's just gonna take time," I assure her. She gives me a small, awkward hug before pulling back.

"What's next?" she asks.

I hold up the warp core. "We've got to get this back."

"Let's go, then." She doesn't sound very excited about it but nevertheless she and I make our way to the Lido Deck. We arrive at the boarded-up entrance, the once-beautiful sign missing several letters and no longer lit up. I peel away the panel I loosened to get in here the first time and we duck into the small hallway with the bulkhead at the other end. My mom suddenly stops short.

"What's wrong?" I ask.

She looks distraught. "I... haven't been here since... then," she says. Now it makes sense why she didn't sound enthusiastic about making this trip up here with me. More than that, it makes sense why she never tried to repair this section of the ship.

"You don't have to come. Seriously, I can do this on my own," I say.

"No, it's fine." Her voice is a little shaky, but she keeps walking. "Let's suit up here," she says, walking over to one of the walls and sliding open a panel, revealing a rack with about a dozen hanging spacesuits.

"Oh, I didn't know those were there," I say. That probably would've saved me trouble last time I was down here. Would've been much easier than stealing one from the bridge, which is what I ended up doing. We pull the suits on and climb into the airlock. I push the button and feel the air leave the room.

We both walk forward into the cafeteria again, the gravity slowly getting weaker as we walk. I look up at the ceiling and see the giant hole, although now it brings up a whole mix of sadness, guilt, and terror. I look back down and notice my mom hasn't looked up once. Her focus seems to be solely on getting to the other side of the room. I can't say I blame her.

We reach the next airlock and quickly move through it into the Lido Deck and breathable air. It looks just like it had when I explored it on my own. The vending machines bob along through the air alongside scattered beach supplies and dishes from the bar. I push off towards the bar and use it to pull myself toward the far wall.

Neither my mom nor I say anything as we find the panel on the wall and enter the guts of the ship. We follow the walkway, ducking under the pipe that had nearly crushed us on the last trip. I see the small room ahead, and when we get inside I take off my helmet and pull the warp core out from inside my suit.

"I don't know how to get it back in," I say. My mom takes off her helmet and gloves, carefully letting them float nearby.

She grabs the warp core from me. "Let me do it."

"You know how?"

"You forget it's been twenty years for me. I've picked up a few things along the way," she says before getting to work. Her hands move quickly as she attaches the warp core back into the pedestal, pulling clumps of wires and tubes together and plugging them one-by-one back into the warp core. It only takes a few minutes until everything has been fully re-integrated.

"Please choose a command," the AI panel chimes to life as my mom closes the top of the pedestal. She taps the option that says START ENGINE and the room fills with the blinding blue light. I feel vibrations pulsing through the air.

"Let's get back up to the bridge." She grabs her helmet and gloves, tugging them back on. We pass through the Lido Deck and the cafeteria without a further word and ditch the spacesuits on our way back up to the bridge. When we arrive there, Iris, Nao, and Egon are already sitting around one of the computers. It reminds me of how they used to be back in the observatory. I guess the only ones missing are Atticus and Masumi.

"We're back," I say.

Iris turns around. "And the warp core?"

"All back in place and running again," my mom says.

"Good, now come see what we found." Iris waves us over and we join the group around the screen. There are a bunch of random maps and stars, but I can't make too much sense of what we're looking at. Iris points to a small dot on the screen. "We found that other signal you picked up from the shuttle."

"Wait, really? What is it?" I ask.

Iris leans in closer to the screen. "Not a clue."

"Any guesses?" my mom asks.

"It could be another ship. Or, if I'm being optimistic, it might even be a settlement," Iris says.

"A settlement?" I ask.

"Yeah, these ships were never intended to be the final stop for us. Remember all the equipment in the observatory? Turns out Atticus' theory was right, it was designed to survey for inhabitable planets," Iris explains.

"So you think one of the other ships managed to find a planet?" my mom asks.

"It's entirely possible," Iris says. They seem to be having a conversation completely on their own. But it's nice seeing them like this again. I can feel some of my mom's energy coming back.

"And what about the ship? Can it handle a warp?" my mom asks.

Iris thinks about it for a second. "Probably just one."

"Well, let's hope one is all we need then." My mom turns back to the rest of the bridge, full of enthusiasm. "Ok, we're going to start disembarkment protocols," she announces. The crew snaps to attention and one of them taps on a panel. The announcement system turns on and I hear a recording of my mom's voice.

"ATTENTION RESIDENTS OF THE *MERCURY*. PLEASE PROCEED TO HABITATS. DISEMBARKMENT PROTOCOL NOW INITIATED." It's the same message as before but she's recorded over my grandmother's voice.

"What else do we need before launching?" she asks Iris.

"Navigation, we need to get it synced with the warp systems," Iris says.

"How long will it take?"

Iris looks over the other consoles around her. "Maybe two hours."

"Good, that'll be enough time for everyone to get to their habitats."

I watch as Iris pulls wires out of the various consoles and hooks them into others. Whatever work she's doing passes completely over my head so I keep out of the way. The two hours seem to fly by with everyone running around getting everything together.

"Ok, I'm going to start the check-in process for the disembarkment ships." My mom walks back over to the helm of the ship and turns on the ship's intercom. "Attention all residents of the *Mercury*. We will now be starting our check-in process with all two-hundred and twenty disembarkment ships. Please ensure that all entrances are completely sealed and all residents are securely seated in their respective drop seats." She flips off the intercom. "Iris, how much longer until we're good to go?"

"I'll be done with it by the time you're finished with your checks," Iris responds from underneath one of the consoles.

My mom nods and flips on the intercom. "Ship DE-001-A. Are you ready to disembark?"

I hear a crackling voice come through from the other side. "This is DE-001-A. Can confirm we are ready at your order, Captain."

My mom makes a check on the screen in front of her and a green box appears. "Ship

DE-001-B. Please confirm your status?" she says next.

"We're all ready, Captain," a new voice says through the intercom. Another check on the screen. Another green box. I watch as my mom moves through the list of disembarkment ships and slowly checks them off.

Iris finally comes out from under the console and flips a switch on. "Nav system's all set, Helena," she says, before walking over to me. "You should really get ready."

I look around, confused as to what I should be doing. "What do you mean?"

"The bridge is going to be our makeshift disembarkment ship," she explains.

"I don't understand." The other ships are nothing like the bridge.

"That's ok, you don't have to. You just have to buckle in," Iris says as she points to the row of seats at the side of the room. I run over to one of the chairs and strap myself in, watching as everyone else follows suit. Egon, Iris, and Nao all strap in next to me. My mom still stands at the helm of the ship.

"Aren't you going to strap in too?" I ask her. She continues checking off the disembarkment ships, but she also pushes a large button on the console in front of her. A panel opens up directly behind her, and a large chair rises from the floor. She sits down and continues to move through the roster. Ok, that was pretty cool. Still dramatic, but in a much better way.

"Ship DE-100-C. Please report your current status," she says.

"We are secure and ready for takeoff here on DE-100-C, Captain," the voice says.

She makes one final check and the entire panel in front of her turns green. "Disembarkment check complete. All crew prepare for warp." She looks around the room to make sure everyone on the bridge is strapped in, then she takes a deep breath and reaches out to the blue button on the console. "Here we go." She presses the button.

I instantly feel the sensation of falling, just like when the shuttle went through its warp. But this time it's magnified by nearly a thousand. The room glows blue as my body stretches out in front of me. I try gasping for air, but to no avail. The noises that I was unable to identify during my first warp are back with a roar. I close my eyes and try to focus on them. They sound like chirping, small soft squeaks, but with everything else going on it's hard to focus on just one noise. Space feels like it's collapsing in on itself. Suddenly there is a loud boom, like the sound of millions of lightning bolts striking at the same time, and everything snaps back to normal.

I take a deep breath, relieved to have air again, and open my eyes. I almost can't believe what I see before me. There's a planet, deep blue in color. Or maybe that's still the blue light from the warp, it's hard to tell.

"Status report!" my mom yells onto the bridge. Iris is out of her seat in a flash and back at the controls. Egon and Nao run over to her as the entire ship suddenly lunges forward, knocking them off their feet.

"What was that?" I yell. No one answers because right after I ask, there's a horrible creaking sound and the ship shakes again.

"Someone tell me what the hell is going on!" my mom shouts.

"There's a planet!" Iris yells.

"What's it doing there?" my mom yells back.

"We don't know," Iris yells. "But we've got bigger issues."

"Oh yeah? Like what?"

But before Iris can respond, the ship seems to give its own answer in the form of more violent shaking and a deafening crack. "The ship is falling apart! When we hit the atmosphere of this planet the force cracked the ship in half," Iris yells.

My mom flips the intercom back on, a look of panic on her face. "DISEMBARK-MENT GO!" she screams into the intercom before turning back to us. "ALL OF YOU BACK IN YOUR SEATS. THIS SHIP IS GOING DOWN."

CHAPTER FIFTEEN

DISEMBARKMENT

I see the bottom half of the ship falling below us, completely detached from the half that we're on. It looks like something has literally taken our entire ship and just ripped it in two, with all the decks torn apart at the seams. The entire bridge shakes as we fall.

"Everyone hold tight! This is gonna be a little rough!" my mom shouts. She's frantically pushing buttons on the console just before there's an explosion that rocks the bridge. Suddenly we seem to be moving much faster. I catch a glimpse out the window and realize what that explosion was; the bridge just separated from the rest of the *Mercury*.

I watch as the ship starts to crumble into pieces. Through them, I see glimpses into familiar decks. The once magnificent trees on the biome deck are now burning to dust as they fall through the sky. The giant statue from the Lido Deck gets crushed by another chunk of rubble. Just like that, every place I've ever known is vanishing.

"The whole ship's falling apart," I say.

Egon leans in to comfort me. "The ship is, but look at that." He points towards the wreckage and I see all the pieces of debris flying outward.

"I don't see anything," I say.

"Look closer, you see all those pieces flying away there?" I nod, trying to focus harder on what he's pointing at. "Those are the other disembarkment ships."

As he says this, it all becomes clear. There are hundreds of objects moving in completely different directions. I watch as the objects begin to glow, likely booting up their engines as they fall. Most seem to be able to get clear of the ship, but I notice a couple that unfortunately end up right underneath the larger chunks of the *Mercury* and disappear into the mass of burning metal.

"We're gonna be on the ground soon! Prepare yourselves for landing," my mom yells across the bridge. I look out over the landscape and see white stretching in every direction. There's a crashing sound outside and I look out the opposite window to see the two halves of the *Mercury* smash into the ground, leaving giant, dark holes in the pure white landscape. I see more, smaller dark spots across the ground where all the other disembarkment ships have started to land.

My mom continues to press buttons on the console as the ground rises up to meet us. There are swirling clouds of something white outside. Suddenly there's a loud THUD as the shuttle connects with the ground and the straps from my chair dig into my chest painfully. There is another crack as the ship finally stops shaking, followed by nothing but silence. Though as I listen, I can hear the muffled sounds of crashing coming from outside.

"Where are we?" I finally ask, breaking the silence. There's a pause before anyone responds.

"I don't know," Iris answers.

"Well, it's a planet, right?" I ask, unbuckling myself from the jump seat.

She hesitates, then nods. "Yeah, it would seem so."

"Everyone back to their stations." My mom, having pulled herself together, takes charge of the situation. Everyone quickly unstraps from their seats and runs back over to their respective stations. "I want to know where we are and what's going on out there."

Iris taps at her console. "We're close to the source of the signal."

"Who's sending it?" my mom asks, not missing a beat.

"Can't tell. It looks like it's about a mile from here," Iris says.

My mom walks over to Iris and asks her the next question quietly, "Do you think it's a colony?"

"I mean, it's logical that another one of the colony ships finally found an inhabitable planet. But we won't know for sure until we find that signal," Iris whispers back.

"Egon, what's it like out there? Will we need suits?" my mom asks. Egon taps on the panel in front of him.

"It appears that the air of this planet is breathable. However, the temperature is way too low. If we're out there for an extended period we'd probably freeze," he says.

"Well, the suits will help with that, won't they?"

He nods. "Yeah, the spacesuits will help for sure, but we still don't know what might be out there."

"We need to find out. And until we do, I don't want anyone else leaving their ships." She flips the intercom on again. "Attention all ships that can hear me. For your own safety, please remain inside your ships until we have fully assessed our current situation," she finishes and turns the intercom back off. "Ok, all of you get suited up and ready to go. We leave in half an hour." She steps down from the helm.

"Y'all have fun with that," Nao says.

"You're not coming?" Iris asks.

"Nah, I'm gonna stay right here," they say, grabbing a seat at one of the chairs near the main console. They avoid eye contact with my mom. I catch Egon's eye and he shakes his head as if to say there's nothing I can do about Nao and my mom right now.

I follow everyone to the back of the bridge where they're pulling out spacesuits. I open a locker and go to pull one out for myself when my mom's hand stops me.

"You're staying here with Nao," she says.

"Like hell I am!" I say loudly.

"This is not an argument. I need to be sure you stay safe," she says with a stern look.

"Yeah, well you don't know that it's any safer in here than out there," I say.

She sighs and looks over at Nao who sits with their back facing all of us. "Fine. But be careful," she says as she grabs a suit for herself. I see a small smile cross her face. "You really are just like him."

Once everyone is suited up, we make our way down to the large airlock on the deck below. The door shuts behind us once we're inside. Iris has a device in her hand with a large screen. Every couple of seconds it lets out a soft beep like the navigation on the ship. The airlock door opens in front of us and a powerful wind rushes inside with a swirl of white material.

It's almost impossible to see outside at first. The white landscape is completely blinding. My eyes adjust and I finally see details. There's a giant dark hole where half of the *Mercury* landed, and beyond it I can see the blurred outlines of the other disembarkment ships. Once the door has fully opened, we carefully walk down the ramp. When I step off, my feet sink into the ground about an inch before hitting something hard and slightly slippery.

"Be careful on this ground. It looks like it might be some kind of ice," Egon says. I slide my foot across the ground and feel how slippery it is. This gives me a brilliant idea. I push off from the ship and let myself glide across the ground.

"Lucy! What are you doing?" my mom shouts after me as I continue to glide forward. I've seen ice on the ship before but never this much of it at once. I wonder if this whole planet is covered in it. My metal foot slips out from underneath me and I fall to the ground, landing softly on the white surface. My balance has gotten better but I guess ice is a little tougher.

That's when I realize what all the flecks of white actually are. It's snow. I've only ever read about it before but seeing it in person is kind of beautiful. "Just having a little fun!" I shout back to her. It's hard to see her expression through the visor of her suit but I assume it's probably not the happiest one. I pull myself back up and glide over to her.

"If you're going to come with us you have to stay close. And no more goofing around. We have no idea what to expect on this planet," she says sternly.

I can feel how stressed she is, so I stop gliding on the ice. She starts walking in the opposite direction from the crash, following closely behind Iris who's already off on her own.

Iris leads the group over the ice with her scanner gripped tightly. I can hear its pings every couple of seconds. I walk carefully to make sure I don't fall, but it turns out that when you're just trying to walk across the ice it's actually a lot harder than gliding across it. The snow blowing in the wind makes it hard to see anything past a couple feet, so our group does our best to stick close together.

"Ok, let's stop here for a second," Iris says. "There's a steep hill in front of us. We're going to need some grips to get up it." She pulls out a small pack and begins attaching metal pieces to the underside of her boots.

Egon walks over and grabs a handful. "Everyone attach these to the bottom of your suit, just be careful not to let them puncture it.

We're not going to be able to walk up this without them," he says. I follow him over to Iris' bag and start pulling out spikes for myself. It's a little tough to grab them through the gloves of the spacesuit but I manage to pick up a couple. They clip right into the bottom of my boots and when I put my feet back onto the ground the metal spikes sink into the ice below.

I walk around in a tight circle. My feet no longer slide at all. "Why weren't we using these the whole time?"

"Because we don't know the structure of this ice beneath us. I didn't want to use them unless absolutely necessary," Iris says.

"And you're sure it's absolutely necessary now?" my mom asks.

"Yes, now let's keep moving," Iris says. She takes off for the hill in front of us and we follow. It's much easier to walk with the added traction. Within ten minutes we near the top of the hill. Admittedly, I'm moving a little slower than some of the others since the cold is making the joints in my metal foot lag. But just as before, Egon hangs back and makes sure I have someone to walk with. Ahead of us, everyone stops when they reach the top of the hill.

When I join them, I immediately see why. Before us is a large, flat stretch of ice, but what's beyond it is far more interesting.

There's a massive hill that reaches up higher than one of the decks, and built into it are a series of large buildings unlike any I've ever seen on the *Mercury*.

"What is that?" I ask.

"It looks like some kind of settlement," Egon says.

"Could that be a colony? It looks old."

"It's hard to tell." Iris looks out over all the buildings. She seems quieter than before.

"Are they the ones who were sending out the signal?" I ask.

She holds up her scanner in the direction of the buildings. "Yes. It does seem to be coming from there."

"Well, let's get over there," my mom says. "And stay alert. We don't know what we're walking into." She begins to walk down the other side of the hill.

Going down is much quicker but I'm still careful not to slide on the ice, even with the spikes on. Once we reach the bottom, we start across the flat stretch toward the buildings.

"We've got about a quarter of a mile left until we reach the other side," Iris says. The pinging from her scanner has been getting progressively louder and more frequent.

As we get closer to the other side of the ice, and now the snow has died down, I can make out the buildings a little clearer. Surprisingly it's not just a couple dozen, it seems like there are hundreds of them, all ascending the large hill. Bright, warm light pours out of every single building and even seems to dot the spaces between.

We reach the edge of the ice and I hear my foot tap against something solid. I take another step and the same thing happens. "What's going on?" I ask.

"It seems this area is no longer an ice sheet. We must have reached a patch of actual ground." Iris looks around and removes the spikes from the bottom of her suit. Following her lead, we all do the same. I look up and notice a series of figures on the hill in front of us. I can't make out their exact shapes but they seem to be getting closer. My mom steps to the front of the group.

"Everyone get behind me and stay calm. Remember, we're the ones who crashed on their planet," she says. I watch as she slowly walks out to meet the figures. They're roughly the same height as us and are all wearing a thick fabric draped around their bodies. The figure closest to my mom stops and unwraps a layer of fabric from its head. It's a woman. She's got a kind face with a couple of wrinkles and looks to be a little older than my mother.

I don't know what to make of this. How are there humans on this planet? The woman turns and looks over our group. Mom raises her arms above her head and places them on her helmet. With a click, she twists the helmet and removes it completely, lowering it beside her.

"Hello! We come in peace!" she yells over to the figure. I almost laugh. That's the most cliché thing you can say when making first contact, right? Like something off an old reel. The woman steps closer and I see her face more clearly. She has very kind eyes that also look completely puzzled by us.

"Who are you?" the woman asks. Wait, they speak English? What's going on here?

"My name is Helena Inez and I am the captain of the starship *Mercury*. Where are we?" she asks.

The other woman continues to look confused. "My name is Jasmine. And this is June." She gestures to the buildings behind us.

Confusion creeps across my mom's face. "This planet is named June?"

Jasmine shakes her head. "No, what are you talking about? This city is named June." This is the most painful conversation I've had to watch in a while.

Thankfully, Iris steps forward and removes her helmet too. "I'm sorry, we're still catching up. What planet are we on?" she asks.

This seems to confuse Jasmine even more. "What other planet would you be on?" she asks. "This is Earth." Silence from everyone.

Wait, like the old Earth? The one that got destroyed?

"I don't understand," I say.

"Don't worry, you're not alone in that," Egon says.

"We picked up a signal from space and followed it here. Did you not send that out?" my mom asks.

"No. I'm afraid that wasn't us," Jasmine says.

My mom turns back to Iris. "They're not from another colony ship?"

Iris seems puzzled. "It would appear not."

"Then where is the signal coming from?" my mom asks.

"It looks like from near that building over there," Iris says. She points to a tall stone building towering above the ice flat behind us.

"What is that building?" my mom asks.

"That's the lighthouse," Jasmine says.

"Do you mind if we check it out?"

Jasmine smiles. "Sure, you just follow the road back up through town and it should take you there."

"Iris, Lucy, you two go check it out. I want to know what's going on here," my mom says before turning to the others. "The rest of you, let's get back to our ships and let the crew know what we've found here."

This seems to catch Jasmine's attention. "Rest of the crew? How many of you are there?"

"Thousands." She pauses and looks back to where the ship crashed. "At least before the crash. We haven't done a full headcount since," my mom says.

Jasmine looks shocked. "I didn't know there were that many people still alive."

"We're going to need to set up some kind of shelter," my mom says.

"We can try to help. But first, we should make a plan to figure out what to do with everyone," Jasmine says. She walks over and places an arm around my mom. "Come back up to my place and we'll figure out how to make this work."

My mom leans in towards Egon. "Egon, you head back to our ship and let everyone know they're going to need to be patient, ok? And try to get a headcount started. That's going to take a while."

"Sure, anything else you want me to tell them?" Egon asks.

"No, not yet. Just to be patient. And, Lucy, please stay safe." She pulls away from Jasmine just long enough to give me a small hug. It's a little awkward but sweet. She gives

me a quick nod before going with Jasmine
back up toward the buildings.

"Let's go check out that lighthouse," Iris
says. She walks along the pathway toward it
and I follow.

The dirt road leads us through the town
and people stare at us from the buildings as
we pass by. There are also a couple of people
walking through the streets nearby. One of
them passes close and I notice it doesn't look
human at all. Well, its face looks human, but
the skin is made from metal. It stares back at
us as we walk past.

"What was that?" I ask Iris as soon as it's
out of earshot.

"I think it's an android," she says. She
seems to be mostly focused on the scanner in
her hand rather than any of the other stuff
around us. "It's like a robot built to help people. They had them back on Earth," she explains. I catch glimpses of more of these an-
droids. Something about them is a little unset-
tling.

The path continues winding forward and
at its end sits the lighthouse. It's a tall, white
building that, like many of the other things
we've passed, looks mostly covered in ice. As
we reach the base, I see a large metal sign
above the door that reads 'WARDEN-
CLYFFE LIGHTHOUSE'. Iris walks up to
the front door and pulls it open.

We step inside and I finally remove my helmet. The room is octagonal with a large spiral staircase in the center. I sneeze loudly. It's very dusty in here. There are a couple of desks stacked with papers around the edges of the room and more bookshelves than I can count. Every inch of the walls is covered in wires that run up from the floor and continue through the ceiling.

"The signal's coming from directly above us." Iris holds the scanner above her head.

The anticipation is killing me. Whatever this signal is, it was strong enough to reach my shuttle light years away from here. I can't even begin to imagine what we're going to find. Iris walks over to the staircase and starts climbing without hesitation. Her feet make a loud noise as she steps onto the first metal stair. I follow her, clanging along loudly behind her.

We arrive on the second floor, which looks very similar to the previous one, lots of papers and books everywhere. It doesn't look like anyone's used it much since the whole room has a thick layer of dust.

"It looks pretty abandoned," I say. Iris doesn't respond, all her attention squarely focused on the scanner. My foot starts to feel sore as we continue to climb each level. I've probably just been standing on it for too long at this point.

The next floor looks completely different, like it was once someone's living space, fully outfitted with a bed on one side, cabinets, and even what looks like a small kitchen. I wonder if someone used to live here years ago. The next two floors both look like some kind of research lab, almost like the observatory. Every surface is covered with technology of some kind. And just like all the other floors, the walls are layered with thick wires and cables stretching up through the ceiling. We arrive at the second-to-last floor and the spiral staircase ends. Instead, I see two sets of stairs at the edge of the room.

All of the cables from the floors below run into the central pillar of the lighthouse, continuing upwards in one massive bunch.

"Those cables must be important, right?" I ask.

Iris' scanner is going wild with sounds in her hand. She runs over to the stairs at the edge and I sprint after her. We emerge into a spherical glass room. The walls are made from large beams of metal with thick glass triangles between them. Around the room are massive white statues, one of which I recognize instantly. It shows a man dressed in a long robe with wings on his feet. It's the same statue from the *Mercury*. The one I've seen in every corner of the ship, from the tiniest gardens to the pillars in the Lido Deck.

"What's that doing here?" I ask. Iris still doesn't seem to hear me. I look closer at the statue. On its base is a metal plaque that says '*MERCURY*'. I look around at the other statues in the room. Each one depicts a different person but they all have similar plaques at their base. I walk around the room looking at each one. '*JUPITER*', '*JUNO*', '*VESTA*'; I've never heard of any of these names before. In total, I count twelve statues.

Iris is standing in front of a door in the center of the room. She has her scanner placed right in front of it. This must be where all those wires converge.

"This is where the signal is coming from," she says.

"What is it?"

"That is what gives us power," a voice from behind us says. I whip around to see Jasmine standing at the top of the staircase, my mother beside her.

"What do you mean? Like this is where your society's political power comes from?" Iris asks.

Jasmine laughs. "No, I was being quite literal. That is the source of all the electrical power on this planet."

How could that possibly be? She walks over to the door and places her hand on it. The door slides open, revealing a young girl sitting on a chair with her eyes closed. She looks peaceful. If I had to guess, I'd say she's a little younger than me. It seems like an odd place to be sleeping.

But perhaps even odder is the panel open on her chest with a glowing red object inside. Wires from all around are plugged into it and red light pulses along them, filling the room with their glow. Maybe it's just my imagination, but the light almost feels warm.

"I don't understand," says Iris.

"Well, there's a first time for everything," I joke.

Jasmine looks over at the girl lovingly. I look at her too and realize that she doesn't seem to be asleep at all. In fact, she doesn't even appear to be breathing. And yet I can clearly see Jasmine's fondness for this girl all over her face. She must have been someone important to her.

"This is Bit," Jasmine says with a smile. "And she's the girl who gave her life to save the world."

Acknowledgements

There are so many people I would like to thank for helping to make Mercury a possibility. I began writing this book around the same time I began Wardenclyffe and it's taken a lot of hard work and polish from a number of people to get it where it is today.

As with everything in life, I would not be anywhere without my incredible mother who was a huge support this past year as I moved to my new home across the country, nearly 3000 miles away! And a special thanks to my entire family for always being so supportive of my creative passions.

To my editor, Jess, who helped me turn the early versions of this story into the polished version you see today. This book would not have been what it is without all your help and guidance.

Thanks to Minna Ollikainen, who, once again, created absolutely beautiful illustrations for each chapter of this story. And thanks to Abigail Spence for painting another stunning cover that makes everyone want to pick up a copy of this book. I am constantly in awe of the beautiful art the two of you create and am so honored to work with you both on these books.

I'd also like to thank my writing group, The Splotches, who helped spark the original idea for this story through their feedback on my first book. And to all the new writing friends I've made this past year in California.

Lastly, I would like to thank everyone who supported my first book, Wardenclyffe. Every single positive review makes my heart feel so full and gave me the motivation to continue working on Mercury. I hope you will enjoy it as much as I enjoyed writing it!

ABOUT THE AUTHOR

Lloyd Hall grew up in a small town on the coast of Connecticut called Short Beach. His childhood was filled with fantastical stories and he often found himself lost in many books from the local library. He channeled his childhood love of stories into his first novel, Wardenclyffe. He is proud to continue the story with the second book in the series, Mercury.

www.lloyd-parker-hall.com